Finding Quetzal

by
Jim & Cheryl Pahz

Finding Quetzal
© Jim and Cheryl Pahz 2013

Published by The Writers' Collective
Mount Pleasant, Michigan

ISBN - 978-0-9886423-24

For Lisa
Who Makes Our Souls Smile

Jim & Cheryl Pahz

1
QUETZAL
PRESENT DAY

My name is **Quetzal Maya Fisher**, but everyone calls me Kat. I was born thirty years ago in Guatemala to a peasant girl named Felicita. I have a photograph of her that Grace gave me. In the photo my mother, Felicita, smiles shyly at the camera as she sits on a bench next to an avocado tree. She is abundantly pregnant with me inside her belly. To me, her face is a mystery; it looks young and hopeful, but also knowing and resigned. What secret was she carrying inside her, along with me? Two days after the picture was taken, I was born.

The place in the photograph is Canoguitas, a rural village in the Guatemalan lowlands, about an hour from the ocean and surrounded by jungle. It is hot and humid in Canoguitas, and I probably wouldn't have survived a childhood there with my asthma. Felicita left the day after I was born. She never held me or even kissed me goodbye. She demonstrated her love in a more costly and complicated way, as is often the case with the poor and desperate. Felicita simply vanished into the jungle, continuing toward her destiny and leaving me to mine.

I was adopted by parents from the United States. Just as Dorothy was abruptly moved from Kansas to Oz, I was plucked from Guatemala and plopped into the middle of Michigan. So it should come as no surprise that I believe in fate—in destiny. How could I not? I don't mean this in a vain way, like I am somehow different or special. I think fate touches us all, but it's often hard to detect. It can be subtle and obvious at the same time, like the intricate designs of Guatemalan embroidery where, stitch by stitch, fate connects our lives and gives substance to our days. I believe there is a code in those colorful threads; a code that determines the design and connects us to others.

In my case, fate was outrageous—a crude device to correct an obvious mistake. Adoption was the expedient way to get me where I properly belonged so the story could go on. I don't think this is saying anything against God. In fact, I feel more secure knowing that the ills of this world are just that—ills and flaws that shouldn't be here, and that God has some tools at His disposal to set things right. I can't believe that right now the world is a perfect place—exactly the way God wants it.

Sometimes the tools of fate are people like you and me. We each contribute, with complete ignorance on our part, to the lives of others. Occasionally, when looking back, we might detect a strange coincidence or an uncanny parallel, but this is usually long after the event has occurred, and we tend to doubt our senses or recollections. A man named Tommy Tuttle was the tool God used in my fate, and actually the fate of many others. My story is very much intertwined with Tommy's. Along with the DNA that shaped my physical being, Tommy's actions brought me to this moment. I doubt Tommy thought about any of this. In his younger years he would have laughed at the idea of being used as an instrument by God or anyone else. He considered himself fully in charge and blatantly used whatever might be at hand—his good looks, charm, and even the Bible—to accomplish his goals. But in the end, God outsmarted him and everything wound up exactly as it should.

You might wonder about Felicita, and I've wondered about her too. I see her every morning when I look in my mirror. I see her every night as I gaze at my daughter and kiss her cheek at bedtime. Felicita is my shadow mother hidden deep inside, who whispers to me in my dreams. I often think of her when I wake up in the night, and I believe she speaks to me. Her photograph is now faded with age—all the color has drained away—but still she sits on the bench in front of the Evangelical Friendship Mission of Guatemala. When I visited the mission, I found her spot, but the bench, sadly, was gone. Felicita came to the mission because of Tommy—a generous man who could change the life of an impoverished young woman and her fatherless infant. He had helped others before. Tommy had magnificent blue eyes. With such eyes anything is possible.

So when I became a detective of fate (my fate), I searched for a beginning... for a magical thread to be my guide. I found it in the Evangelical Friendship Mission of Guatemala, which wasn't really a surprise. I'd heard about the mission my whole life growing up in Michigan. The directors were household names. Every year our families exchanged holiday cards, and my parents always made an annual contribution to the mission. My parents are not religious people, but their ties to the Tuttles were strong. My dad went to college with Grace and Tommy, and once he even asked Grace to marry him. Fortunately Grace declined. Knowing Grace and knowing my dad, it would have been a terrible match. Instead Grace married Tommy and the two of them, with very different motives, went to Guatemala to take their places at the mission Tommy's father had started two decades before. Tommy's father was Lester Tuttle, the evangelist and missionary.

The surprise for me was learning about the adoption scandal. I knew nothing about it until

I began my research. I discovered it in an old newspaper clipping from the *Miami Herald* dated a year after I was born. My parents never discussed it that I can recall. I saved the clipping, of course. It's fragile now, like the photograph of Felicita... like the threads that connect our lives.

"An American missionary in Guatemala was arrested in an alleged kidnapping ring. Police raided a house operated by the Evangelical Friendship Mission of Guatemala and arrested the directors: Mrs. Lila Tuttle and her stepson, Mr. Tommy Tuttle. Police seized six children ranging in age from one week to ten years. According to children's rights worker, Elida Hernandez, Guatemala has ineffective laws regulating adoptions. Hernandez said that 'some people make money by trafficking in babies put up for adoption to foreign couples.' The investigation of the Tuttles began when a 24 year-old woman claimed her son had been taken without permission and sold to Mr. Tommy Tuttle. Upon investigation, it was determined that many of the children housed in the facility lacked the proper documentation to satisfy legal requirements...."

That was the beginning of my detective work and the long process of reclaiming the faded and tattered tapestry of my past. To bring back the vivid design, I became a hunter seeking a long-vanished trail. The skills needed to track the invisible are many: determination, memory, imagination, and (above all) intuition. Along the way a strange thing happened. The hunter and the hunted merged; we became as one to the extent that I could remember and recognize what in actuality I never experienced or saw. But the truth I found was real to me, as real as the photograph of Felicita on the bench in Canoguitas. In the end that is all that matters. That is all there is: our truth, our story, as only we can know it.

2
THE BEGINNING
NOVEMBER 1945

In the courthouse of a Midwestern city, across from the Hotel Aurora, sat two men convicted of involuntary manslaughter and child endangerment. A six-year-old boy had perished in a house fire. The prosecutor alleged the men had been intoxicated at the time of the fire, and he characterized their behavior as criminally reckless. Shaking his head, he solemnly asserted, "And neither of them has expressed any remorse or responsibility for their actions and the subsequent death of this child."

The older defendant, 28-eight-year old Lester Tuttle, sat stiffly in the new shirt and slacks his mother had provided for the occasion. He looked both defiant and humbled. Lester was lean with angular features and rough hands that didn't know how to lie still in his lap. His most striking feature was his voice, which was low with an intimate quality like a cat purring in the dark. As a child he had been troubled by his voice because it felt too big for him. It made him seem older than he was, and people always expected him to say something smart. Even now he could not live up to his voice. It was like a musical instrument he couldn't master and this troubled him.

Given the opportunity to make a final statement, Lester began by reciting a passage he found in the Bible that had been placed in his jail cell. He hoped a religious reference would reflect well on him and help his situation. He had memorized the passage from the *Book of Isaiah*: *None calleth for justice, nor any pleadeth for truth....* Lester began well, but then faltered. Standing in the courtroom he failed his voice once again. Overcome with fear and apprehension, Lester couldn't recall the rest of the verse. His mind went blank. After an awkward pause he gave up on the verse and continued in his own words: "I don't understand all this. You acquit the guilty and condemn the innocent. Well, maybe I'm not so innocent, but I ain't so guilty either—not like you make me out to be. I can swear to that. But I guess you gotta do what you gotta do. Anyway, this whole thing stinks if you ask me. It's wrong... all wrong." Then he shrugged and slumped back onto the wooden seat in defeat. Lester was used to defeat.

****

A young woman named Penny Ellis watched the proceedings at Lester Tuttle's hearing. Only a few months away from having her first child, she sat with her hands cradling the base of her sizeable belly. She was a large woman and was enjoying her pregnancy. For the first time in her life she didn't have to apologize for being overweight. Still, the prospect of actually having the baby, as opposed to being pregnant with it, filled her with apprehension. Under different circumstances she would be thrilled about becoming a mother. But the father of her child, Lester Tuttle, sat at the front of the courtroom listening to the judge. Her baby's father would likely go to prison for a crime she was sure he didn't commit. If Lester was incarcerated, what would she do? Penny stared at the back of Lester's head, trying to memorize the color and texture of his hair—it was a light brown and somewhat coarse, reminding her of shredded wheat.

The judge leaned forward and addressed the court, stating in a matter-of-fact voice that sentencing would occur on January 29th. Then he dismissed the proceedings. Penny grasped her belly as Lester was led from the courtroom. *Good Lord,* she thought. *What will happen to us? What's to become of me and the baby?* In response to her silent prayer, the answer flashed through her mind. She would do the only thing she knew how to do. She would wait. No matter how bad things got, she would wait for Lester. He and their baby were all she had.

****

Lester felt as if someone had punched him hard in the stomach. He found it difficult to move as he was handcuffed and led from the court to be returned to the county jail where he and his friend, Russell, would remain until sentencing. Without thinking, Lester began to pray. He hadn't been to church in several years, but he had been quite religious as a boy. Grasping for the comfort he knew as a child, Lester asked God for the patience of Job and the strength of Samson, so he might endure the fate that lay before him.

The event that had landed Lester in court was a tragedy; on this, Lester and the judge were in agreement. But Lester did not feel responsible for the fire that took Larry's life. Nor was he indifferent to the child's suffering and death, as the prosecutor suggested. Larry was Lester's nephew. He had been a mischievous six-year-old who could spit like a baseball player and loved to hunt insects in the vacant lot across the street. Lester loved Larry and he was now haunted by images of the child, with his rosy cheeks and dirty fingernails, collecting grasshoppers in a jar or hopping down the dusty driveway with Sparkey, the little spaniel, yapping at his feet. Lester knew that Larry was responsible for the fire. On previous occasions he had caught his nephew playing with matches and he had warned his sister to keep an eye on the boy. But when Lester mentioned this to the police, Sharon screamed and called him a liar and coward. Lester couldn't defend himself without accusing Larry, and such accusations made Lester look suspicious and untrustworthy. When he defended himself, Lester felt small and weak, as if he was abandoning or sacrificing Larry.

During the trial, a parade of people had taken the witness stand to testify against Lester. He didn't recognize some of the people, but they all claimed to know him. They said he drank and gambled, which was true. They described Lester as lazy and irresponsible because he didn't have a steady job and moved around a lot. Lester couldn't deny what these people said, but why should it matter when he wasn't drunk at the time of the fire? Yes, he had moved a lot since high school, but he always paid his own way. He hadn't found his place in the world yet, but that didn't mean he was no good, did it? He explained this to his attorney, confident justice would prevail. But Mr. Hart slowly shook his head and informed Lester that when a child dies, jurors have trouble seeing the truth—and it didn't help that Sharon, his flesh-and-blood sister, was against him. No one was interested in Lester or his truth. Lester asked to speak in his own defense, but Mr. Hart advised against it saying, "That's a bad idea, Lester. It might make things worse." *Worse?* Lester now wondered how things could possibly be any worse. He had lost more than his precious nephew in the fire—he had also lost his sister. In fact, the only member of his family to offer any support was his mother, and he suspected she remained by his side more out of loyalty than belief in his innocence.

By the time of sentencing, Lester was prepared for the worst. He was no longer sure what was right or wrong. He only knew this truth: a perfect six-year-old boy was gone forever, and he, a crude and worthless sinner, remained. A child had died and someone had to pay. There was nothing fair about Larry's death; there was nothing fair about Lester's sentence. Fairness was not to be expected. It was an illusion that veiled a world of adversity and allowed mothers and fathers to sleep at night and dream of a better tomorrow.

****

During his initial weeks in prison, Lester felt forsaken and cold. He had never liked Ohio winters because he was sensitive to the cold. Now he shivered every night in his sleep and yearned for a long, hot soak in his mom's big tub. When he shared the story of Larry's death with the other inmates, all nodded in sympathy. They understood it was all a big mistake because they were also victims of mistakes. The prison seemed to be filled with people who had been wrongfully convicted; the whole population was there, apparently, because of miscarriages of justice.

There wasn't much to do in prison except think… and wait… and listen. His thoughts often wandered to Penny Ellis, who had stood by him and never questioned his innocence. Before his imprisonment, Lester had not appreciated Penny, and, even though she was pregnant with his child, he never considered her as girlfriend material. She was little more than trash; someone to mess around with. But during the cold nights as he huddled under his scratchy wool blanket, he saw Penny in a different light. Even though she was slightly overweight, she still appeared feminine and graceful. "Motherly" and "capable" were words that came to mind when he thought of her. Such thoughts made him feel safe and warm. And then, two months into his sentence, she gave birth to a little boy—his son. She named the baby Joseph, after her father, and sent Lester a photograph of a surprised little face peering out from under a blue knit hat. Penny regularly sent letters with pictures and stories of Joseph, sharing the small details of life outside prison. These letters were a bright spot in Lester's life, and he enjoyed looking at them over and over. They were all he had and they made him feel good.

Eventually Lester was given work assignments within the prison walls. He did cleaning work and prepared meals. Later, because of his good behavior and cooperative attitude, he was assigned to work details outside the prison grounds. He mulched branches and dry brush at the wastewater treatment facility in Mount Sterling, and he helped maintain the Fayette County soccer field. He even picked up litter along Route 83 and helped with cleanup at the Ohio State Fairgrounds. Lester liked keeping busy, especially with anything that got him outside the prison. He found it easier to get through the day if he kept busy. At night he would lie on his cot and escape into thoughts of Penny and Joey. He envisioned a life outside of prison and imagined himself as a husband and a father. In his fantasies he eagerly took out the garbage to a shiny pail that never got too full, and he pushed Joey on a sturdy swing set—the kind whose feet were firmly cemented into the ground. Such thoughts brought him comfort. And then the unthinkable happened. One day Lester received a letter from Penny. The envelope was smaller than usual and there were no photographs of Joseph. Curious, Lester read:

My Dear Lester,

I can hardly bear to write these words. Two days ago our precious Joseph was called home to be with our Lord and Savior. He died in his sleep. The doctor says this sometimes happens, especially with boys. They don't know why. My heart hurts so; I don't believe I can hold all the pain I feel. I am sorry to bring this news to you. Even though you never held Joey, I know you loved him. There is no knowing why this horrible thing happened. Pastor Martin said our little boy was so precious to God that our Lord wanted him to be close by. I hope our beloved baby is happy now, as he is with his Lord. God bless and keep you, Lester. I pray for you every day. I miss you and Joey so much I can hardly bear it.

With Love,
Penny

Lester just sat on his cot for a long time

staring at Penny's letter. Then he gathered all the photographs he had of Joseph and spread them on his cot. He rearranged the pictures several times, as if trying to complete a jigsaw puzzle. "You win," he said as he looked at the pictures of Joseph. "Do with me what you will, cause I can't go on." His cell now seemed colder than ever, and he was overcome by the despair he felt with Joseph erased from his future.

It just goes to show, he thought, *no matter how bad things are, they can always get worse. What's next?* His son had been taken from him before he ever held him or looked into his eyes. Two innocent children were dead, while he, Lester, still lived. Why? What had he done to deserve such punishment?

****

A month after Joseph's death, Lester received a letter from his mother. It wasn't the first letter she had sent, but this time she informed him that she had enrolled him in a mail-order Bible study course offered through Renewal Ministries of Georgia.

The next week an envelope with the first Bible lesson arrived. Lester didn't open it immediately, but it did intrigue him. He felt the pleasant stirring of anticipation as he held the envelope, and the physical sensation so moved him that he actually smiled several seconds as he savored the feeling. He had once been religious like his mother, back when he was a boy and together they attended the Solid Rock Church of the Pentecost. It was after his father left, and Lester became the man of the house. Even though he was younger than his sister, Sharon, he was afforded special privileges as the only male child. He went to Bible camp every summer and had his own Bible with his name embossed on the brown leather cover. He became quite good at reciting Bible verses, which won him the approval of the congregation and a silver medal award five years straight. That was before he "went wild" (as his mother described it) and stopped attending church. It was before he started drinking and skipping school. Thinking about those early days, before he lost his way, made Lester feel better—as if he were reconnecting with a lost friend.

Every day for a week, Lester would take out the unopened envelope that held the Bible lesson and study it. He wanted to be spiritually ready before he opened it. When Sunday came and he knew it was time, he opened the envelope and began to read the lesson and answer the questions. He sent it back to the ministry, and about two weeks later he received his first assignment back, corrected, along with lesson two. Lester had been eagerly anticipating its arrival, and he was excited to find out how well he scored. This time he opened the envelope immediately and saw that he ranked in the eighty-fifth percentile.

By the time Lester was released from prison, he had successfully completed two Bible correspondence programs, and he had become a lay minister. Lester discovered that he liked helping people, and he had a feeling for the Word. He decided that for the remainder of his time on earth, he would invite the Holy Spirit into his life and let God direct his path. *Where He leads me, I will go*. Lester was determined to apply himself to whatever challenges were before him. In prison, Lester had reached the conclusion that God was not punishing him, but testing him. God had closed one door (the door on his sinful and selfish ways) but opened another (to a life of love, sacrifice, and service).

As soon as he was released from prison, Lester married Penny at the Solid Rock Church of the Pentecost. His mother watched proudly as he and Penny pledged their love to one another and later when they committed their lives to God. Their intent was to do missionary work wherever the Lord would lead them. Lester addressed the congregation one morning, asking them to pray for him and Penny, and if the Lord spoke to their hearts, to pledge financial support.

"I am not sure where we are going," he said, "but I am certain we are going someplace. I know there are people who promise to go overseas and work for the Lord, but never actually go. That is not us. We are committed; we will go." Lester shared the story of the tragic fire that had changed his life. "God closed many doors in my life. That was my fault, not God's fault. I was back-slid and I was punished for it. That's what it took to get my attention! Finally, when it seemed there were no doors left, I looked around and found the one door I was meant to walk through all along. Everything happens for a reason. That door I walked through led to my wonderful wife, Penny. And today it has led me to you. You can help open the next door that God wants us to enter, and we will walk through it together."

Lester led the congregation in prayer, asking God to have mercy on him and to give him the courage to do His will. And lastly he prayed that those whom God called upon would open their hearts and wallets and pledge their financial support.

"Remember, God is served in many ways. Please don't turn away as I did when God comes knocking on your door. Believe me, when God calls, in one way or another, He *will* get your attention."

Lester had finally mastered his voice. People listened and they began making pledges. Enthusiasm grew so high that Pastor Martin helped Lester set up an account for the Tuttle Missionary Fund. He urged Lester to become associated with a mission board and speak at other churches. Lester followed his pastor's advice and he spoke at any church that would have him. This practical experience rounded out his Bible study certifications. For two years, Lester and Penny traveled the Midwest, addressing church groups of various denominations. Each time Lester spoke, he gave his personal testimony. He told about the fire and how little Larry had perished. He spoke of the strength of the two women in his life—his saintly mother and his devoted Penny—who had been the only ones, besides Jesus, to offer comfort and stand by him. He described the anguish of being a father separated from a son he was never able to hold. Then he revealed how God spoke to his heart as he languished behind prison bars in a state of despair. At the end, he looked out at the upturned faces in the congregation while Penny watched from her chair at the side of the pulpit.

"I know you've heard this before, but it's

worth repeating. The Lord," Lester said, "works in mysterious ways. Sometimes it's beyond our understanding. But sometimes it's clear as day. All I am certain of is that He is leading me in the right direction—to you!" And Lester would point his finger directly at someone sitting in the front pew. "And you!" he would say a little louder, picking out another face in the congregation. "And you! Together we will make a difference."

By now he was pointing both hands and his voice continued to grow until finally it filled the room, and people were on their feet, clapping and shouting, "Amen!" and "Praise the Lord!"

"Thank you, Lord," Lester cried, looking up toward the ceiling with his arms outstretched as tears slid down his cheeks. And he sincerely meant every word. Lester was truly thankful because he had finally learned to use his voice. He could speak forcefully when he turned his voice over to God, and he was happy to give God all the credit. He thanked the Lord for Penny. Prison, he proclaimed, although terrible, had been the best thing to happen to him, and he was ready to follow wherever the Lord led.

The year 1949 arrived full of promise. Lester and Penny had another son, whom they named Tommy. That was the year the mission board decided to start a program in Central America.

Lester and his family would move to Guatemala—
the land of eternal spring. Lester could not have
been happier. He would never be cold again.

3
BITS AND PIECES

Most of what I know about Lester comes from Grace, his daughter-in-law. She described him to me as a man who was determined, devout, and a bit vain. In the early years of the mission, Lester was susceptible to flattery, and many young, ambitious women used this weakness to their advantage.

By the time I met Lester, he was an elderly great-grandfather confined to a wheelchair. There was always a blanket on his knees or close by because, even in the heat of the Guatemalan jungle, he chilled easily. Like a delicate, prized orchid, he was hourly moved in his wheelchair to follow the sun across the courtyard. With each move he was offered tea, juice, or water along with a variety of tempting fruits and cookies. The woman who pushed him around was his granddaughter. She carried a small piece of cloth and would wipe his chin when he drooled. Lester showed little interest in the beauty of his surrounding or ministrations of those attending to his care. He sat motionless with his eyes closed and his face stretched toward the sun. An observer might think him lost, oblivious to this world. But then a peacock would honk, and a smile would bloom on Lester's face.

From Grace I received stories and photographs of my past, always presented in simple, dispassionate terms. She told the facts as she knew them without embellishment. She was not distracted by her own feelings regarding an event, and she didn't try to fill in the blank spaces. I was twenty-nine years old when Grace gave me the picture of Felicita taken just before I was born.

From my birth mother I received a Saint Christopher medal and a small notebook filled with strange writings. When I was able to read the notebook, I found it contained recipes, instructions for living, and magic spells. The magic was for big events in life, such as how to find peace in the afterlife or how to tell if your spouse is being unfaithful. The notebook was written in a combination of Spanish and Quiche, so it took some time to decipher. Quiche is one of the languages of the indigenous people of Guatemala, the Maya. There are passages which still remain undecipherable after all these years. My adoptive parents, Daniel and Mia, gave me the book and the Saint Christopher medal on my thirteenth birthday. They had shown these things to me before, but when I was sixteen I got to keep them myself in a special wooden box in my room.

In the box there is also a peacock feather which came from my mother, Mia. The feather is from one of the peacocks at the mission where she stayed with Grace while I was being adopted. I love the feather because of what it represents to me— the eye of an artist. Mia was an artist who created collages and sculptures from seemingly unrelated items. Today this is called art from found objects, but she began creating this way long ago, before I was even born. In her work an old watch face might share the stage with buttons, broken dolls, lost keys, and old fishing lures. As if by magic, with the addition of color and texture, there emerges a perfectly recognizable scene of a child fishing on a summer day. Her art bypasses the eye and goes straight to the soul, and when you see the fish and the child, and the clock-face sun, you can't help but smile... the way Lester smiled when he heard the honk of the peacock.

Jim & Cheryl Pahz

4
GUATEMALA
1959

By the time Tommy Tuttle was ten years old, he knew almost everyone in Canoguitas, a sleepy little village in the province of Escuintla, Guatemala, surrounded on all sides by jungle. It was here that Lester and Penny began their missionary work, and for nine years it was Tommy's home. The Tuttles began their project by purchasing one hundred acres of land in quetzales for the equivalent of five hundred dollars. The land was located at the edge of town. A side street without a name meandered through a neighborhood of stucco houses and shacks made of wood, each structure more meager than the one before, until the road abruptly stopped and the jungle began. The land the Tuttles bought had a well, a one-room cement hut, and a stream that ran diagonally across the property. The stream emptied into the Rio Coyolate which was also the name of the only named street in the village, the main thoroughfare.

Life had been difficult at first, and the villagers watched in bewildered amusement as the gringos settled in. Lester, Penny, and Tommy lived in two tents while they worked on the hut. One tent was for sleeping and one for supplies. Cooking and eating were done outside under a canvas canopy suspended by rope tied to a grouping of trees. Their red and white station wagon was parked at the edge of the property just off the road. It faced outward as if it was a lookout guarding the premises. The weather was hot and humid, and initially most of their daily living was done under the canopy, which protected them from the sun and the showers during the rainy season that began in May. Villagers frequently took walks down Calle Coyolate, turning off at the unnamed road to get a glimpse of the foreigners and watch their progress.

The Tuttle compound started small, with a fence surrounding the well, hut, canopy, and tents. The fence was the first item built because the neighborhood pigs were a nuisance. The villagers let the pigs wander freely with a type of twig yoke tied around their necks to keep them from rooting gardens or barging through doorways. The animals had taken a liking to the Tuttles' supply tent, so Lester and Penny built a three-foot tall fence from trees and shrubs Lester cut down to clear the property. The larger, sturdy branches were used as fence posts, which Lester planted in the ground. Penny took the thin branches and twigs and wove them in and out between the posts, making a waddle. A twig gate was fashioned from two four-foot sections that could swing open or be closed and tied shut in the middle.

As the Tuttles worked, Tommy would play—often at the front of the compound where he could watch as people, pigs, and chickens approached. His friendly manner and blue eyes attracted attention. The villagers nicknamed him "the beautiful gringo." They would bring their own children to the edge of the compound. Lester and Penny would smile at the visitors and offer them tea or coffee. At first the villagers were hesitant and shy. The Tuttles later learned their neighbors had been wary for fear they might be asked for identification. In Guatemala, giving personal information could be dangerous. They might be conscripted into the military or some other misfortune could happen. The mere presence of the unusual foreigners aroused suspicion.

Some villagers thought the Tuttles were Jehovah's Witnesses, but Lester explained that wasn't so. He told them that they were independent evangelical missionaries. As time passed, the people began to see that the heart of the gringo family was in the right place. Curiosity turned to respect and gradually to friendship.

When Lester first arrived in Guatemala, his knowledge of Spanish was rudimentary, obtained from the language records and books he studied the year before the move. By the end of the first year in Canoguitas, he could converse adequately. For Tommy, Spanish was his first language. Penny was the slowest to learn Spanish, and never seemed to give it much effort. Over time, the compound grew steadily. The cement hut expanded to four rooms; the tents were gone and replaced by other simple structures: a church, a school, and a clinic. These were hand-made with trees from the land, labor from their neighbors, and the roofs were thatch. The school and the church didn't have pane-glass windows, just openings so that birds and other creatures frequently joined the gatherings.

The most complete and impressive structure was the clinic. It was made of concrete blocks, and had three rooms. One was the main room that served as headquarters for the missionary work. In it were two office desks, a tall file cabinet, and worktables with benches. Off the main room were two smaller rooms. One was an examination room where a visiting doctor or dentist could examine and treat patients. The other was a large storeroom where medicines, equipment, and donations were kept. Various church groups would send items such as clothing, books, canned and dried foods, and toys for children. These would be distributed to members of Lester's congregation as well as to needy families in the village and surrounding jungle. Lester named his program the Evangelical

Friendship Mission of Guatemala.

Lester would preach a sermon to the congregation on Sunday mornings and Wednesday nights. Tommy recited Bible verses in both Spanish and English. Penny played the guitar and tried to teach hymns. With her terrible Spanish, the people sometimes thought her efforts were a comedy routine. They would laugh and Penny laughed with them, not having any idea why they were laughing. On weekdays Lester ran the clinic and taught English to anyone wanting to learn. Penny organized sewing and playgroups for the women and children. Over time, villagers came to trust Lester and Penny. The Americans seemed sincere and generous, and understood the outside world of Guatemala City and beyond. Families came to Lester with problems and Lester would listen and try his best to help. He would send photographs and progress reports to his supporters in the United States, and donations continued to flow along with visitors from the churches to witness and document the good works. At Christmas, every child who entered the church would receive a present and a blessing.

As Tommy grew older, he assisted his parents in many ways. He would run errands or deliver messages on his bicycle, distribute the fliers his father printed, and sometimes act as interpreter, because he was more comfortable speaking Spanish than English. Although he was of average height for a ten-year-old American child, he felt grown up in Canoguitas. Almost everyone other than his parents was shorter than he was. His dark hair contrasted with his blue eyes, and the sun turned his light olive skin a deep golden tan. All the time he lived in Canoguitas, he remained "the beautiful gringo" and, as Lester's son, he felt like a little prince.

His kingdom was a vivid world of reds, oranges, and all hues of purples and greens. Hibiscus, gardenias and poinsettias blazed brightly and spilled in abundance from window boxes, along fences and over walls. Pigs and dogs wandered the streets, and in the compound yard guineas, chickens, and peacocks freely roamed. Avocados, bananas, and coconuts grew in abundance, just waiting to be picked. As he rode his bicycle through Canoguitas, Tommy's senses were bombarded: a sky as wide and blue as the Mediterranean atop the lush green mountains, the sun like a warm hand on his back, and the wind as tender as a kiss carrying the smell of tropical fruit like cushiness and mangos, bananas ripening on the trees mingled with the aroma of tortillas and spices from the kitchens. At the time he didn't realize it, but he was happy in Canoguitas, the village whose name translated as "little canoes." All Tommy knew was that he was where he belonged. Canoguitas was home. It was a warm, friendly community. In the small houses and little shacks, people slept in hammocks. Nobody closed their doors and people left their belongings and went off to work in the fields knowing when they returned their property would be just where they had left it. And then one night everything changed.

Tommy awoke in the dark to a loud wailing sound that he had never heard before. It ruptured the stillness and brought him out of his bed. He shared a room with his sister, Tammy, and she was huddled under the covers with her pink bunny. Tammy had been born in Guatemala and was four years old. She closely resembled her mother, and was not considered a "beautiful one." Her hair was a light-brown-mouse color and her pale skin did not tan. She would get red. A small and frail child, she stayed indoors much of the time with Penny.

"What was that?" Tammy asked, too afraid to get out of bed.

"Dunno," Tommy answered quietly moving toward the front of the hut. He was almost to the doorway when he stopped in his tracks. He heard a car door slam and then an engine grind hesitantly, until it suddenly caught. *No doubt about it,* Tommy thought, *that's Daddy's car.*

As the car turned past the house and onto the road, the headlights momentarily lit the front room where Tommy stood only a few feet from the door. Then darkness fell once again, like a thick blanket. Tommy moved to the door and looked outside in time to see the rear lights of the car swallowed by the blackness as the car rounded a curve. Tommy thought it might be a dream, but then the wailing continued. The sad sound, full of hopelessness and pain, was coming from the clinic. As Tommy stepped through the door, he jumped when something touched his thigh. It was Tammy, clutching her bunny in one hand and his pant leg in the other. Without saying anything the two of them carefully walked across the courtyard to the clinic.

When they entered the clinic, the first thing Tommy noticed was Penny sitting on the floor, her back against the wall. Files and fliers were strewn on the floor around her. Penny's face was red and tear streaked, and when she saw her children she began to cry with complete abandon, causing Tammy to begin crying also. Tommy slowly walked around the room looking at the mess. *Something is very wrong.*

Back in the house, he made his mother tea as she had requested. He also poured a cup for himself. When Penny calmed, she broke the news. "We're going back to Ohio," she said, "without

Daddy." It was then that Tommy began to cry.

"I don't want to go," he said. "I hate Ohio."

Penny dabbed her eyes and then blew her nose. "I'm sorry, but we have to."

"Why?" Tommy demanded. "It's not fair! I want to talk to Daddy."

"This is what your dad wants. There's nothing to talk about."

"I don't believe you. Dad will never leave Canoguitas."

"He's not leaving Canoguitas," Penny stated. Her voice was flat and weary. "We are. It's what he wants."

The next morning Penny began to pack, and Tommy watched as his kingdom was dismantled. He kept expecting his father to pull up in the station wagon, saying everything was all right; it was all a big mistake. If only he could see his father before they left, he knew he could straighten this all out. *I belong in Canoguitas, not Ohio,* he thought as he filled the suitcases with books and clothes. *Daddy needs me.*

But his father never showed up, and after three days it was time to leave. The house was clean and all the papers on the clinic floor had been put away. "What about the May frogs? I was waiting for them." Tommy had been looking forward to the arrival of the rainy season when hundreds of large

frogs would appear out of nowhere. They were
known as May frogs since they appeared in the
month of May. At night the streets would be filled
with frogs, a delight to Tommy and other children.

"There are frogs in Ohio," his mother
answered.

"But what about my baseball bat and Molina?
What about my chicken, Molina?"

"We don't have room," Penny answered.
"They'll have to stay; even Molina."

In a strange way this gave Tommy some
consolation. It made him feel as if part of him was
staying. It gave the sense that someday soon he
might come back for all the things that were here
waiting for him. It was still dark outside on the
morning they left. A pickup truck pulled up, and
a man helped Penny put the suitcases and boxes
in the back of the truck. Then everyone squeezed
inside the cab and they began the journey to Puerto
Barrios where they would board a ship to Miami
and then a bus to Ohio.

"Where is Daddy?" Tammy asked. "I want
Daddy."

"He's in Guatemala City on business,"
Penny said. "He can't come with us now. He has
important work to do." Penny wiped her eyes with
a tissue.

Every time Tommy or Tammy mentioned

their dad, Penny started to cry. It was not the loud wailing cry they heard on the first night, but a silent, wet sobbing that wouldn't cease. Penny seemed filled with a river of pain. She carried a box of tissue with her wherever she went.

All the way to Ohio, Tommy tried to comprehend the new turn of events in his life. *Is Dad mad at me? Did I do something wrong?* The bus ride to Ohio was long and uncomfortable. Penny slept through most of it. Periodically she got off at a stop to go to the bathroom and gave Tommy money to buy food. "Get me a Coke and Twinkie," she'd say, "or a Snowball." When Tammy was awake she either whined or chattered to Pinky, her stuffed bunny. Tommy ignored her by looking out the window at the landscape, and watched as it became increasingly ugly. All the sun and color were draining from life right before his eyes. He was now in a world of grays where the land was flat and the trees didn't appear to have leaves. The snow was dirty, and everyone looked pale and unhappy. Ohio was where Penny's family lived, and her parents, Grandpa Joe and Grandma Mildred, had agreed to help until Penny could get settled.

It had been five years since Tommy last saw his grandparents, but he vaguely remembered them. They were large gray people who smelled funny—not in a particularly good way. "Welcome home," they said as they hugged Penny and smiled at Tommy and Tammy. "You're home now." But Tommy didn't think so. It didn't matter what these grandparents said, home was a place in Tommy's head. Home was where his bicycle would forever lean against the fence and his chicken, Molina, would free-range through his memories. His home was safe where no one could ever take it away from him again.

5
OHIO

When Tommy arrived in Ohio, it was March. It was supposed to be springtime, but the temperature was cold and snow was on the ground. None of them had winter clothes. Penny and Tammy didn't want to leave the house, so Grandpa Joe and Grandma Mildred took Tommy to help with the clothes shopping. The first stop was Woolworth's, where they bought socks, pajamas and slippers for everyone. Since Tommy would be starting school, they also purchased a notebook, paper, pencils, and a lunchbox with a dog on the front named Rin Tin Tin. Next they went to the Goodwill store for the rest of their clothes. First they found three outfits for Tommy. He got to pick out his own winter jacket, and he chose blue because it was bright and reminded him of the sky at Canoguitos. He tried the jacket on, and Grandma Mildred nodded approvingly. "What a beautiful color with your eyes! It looks so nice on you, and it really is in good shape. I don't think this jacket has ever been worn. Now," his grandmother continued, "can you help pick out some things for Tammy and your mother? I am sure you can be a big help. I bet you know all the colors they like."

Tommy nodded, and Grandma led him to

the women's section. Penny had written down all the necessary sizes on a piece of scrap paper, and Tommy's grandmother told him what number to look for on the clothes. Shopping at the Goodwill reminded Tommy of the donation room at the clinic. He was used to sorting through items and looking for the gems others had discarded. They left the store with three big bags of clothes, and Tommy got to wear the blue jacket home. When they arrived, Penny and Tammy were seated exactly where they had been when Tommy had left, but the television show they were watching had changed; it was now something called *Beat the Clock*.

"Thank goodness for Tommy," his grandmother said as she set the bag she was carrying on the floor. "He was so much help."

Grandpa Joe nodded in agreement and patted Tommy on the shoulder. "Indeed he was. You should be very proud of him. He's a fine young man."

"Yeah," Penny agreed as she stared at the television set. Penny took up one end of the couch, and Tammy was asleep under a blanket at the other end. There were two other chairs in the living room, which were the ones his grandparents sat in. Tommy had not found a spot for himself yet, but no one seemed to notice. He gathered up his bag of clothes and the school items, and went to the bedroom he was told was his. There were three bedrooms in the house, and he got one all to himself. Penny and Tammy shared the second spare bedroom.

Tommy's room was small and had been his grandmother's sewing room. She didn't sew much these days because of her arthritis. The sewing machine was folded into itself and looked like a desk. This pleased Tommy, because he intended to write some letters. He had to get a letter out to his father. He took a sheet of paper from his notebook. There must be a way to correct this situation. He wrote:

Dear Daddy,

There was a mistake. Mommy took us away to Ohio. It was a long trip. We had to go by boat and bus. Tammy cried. Mommy said you were mad and we had to leave. I think she is wrong. You are not mad at us, are you? Please write to her or telephone and tell her it was a mistake. We can come home. Ohio is not a good place. It is cold and I don't like it. I feel like I am in jail. Grandma and Grandpa are nice. How is Molina? She is a good chicken. Please take

*care of her until I come home. There are
supposed to be frogs in Ohio, but I haven't
seen any. Write soon.*

Love Tommy

During the first three months, Tommy
wrote several letters. The first thing he would do
after school each day was ask if the mailman had
delivered anything from Guatemala. After three
months with no reply, he continued to write, but he
was less hopeful. He no longer expected a response,
but had gotten into the habit of documenting the
mounting indignities that had become his life.

In Ohio, Tommy no longer felt big or safe
as he had in Canoguitas. Everywhere he looked
people were bigger than he was—especially in
school. Tommy was ridiculed because of the clothes
he wore, because of the lunches his grandmother
packed, and because he wasn't familiar with
the workings of the school. Everything about
classroom life was new to him. Most of all he
was teased about his mother. Penny weighed two
hundred and fifty pounds and was growing. Her
days were spent on the couch watching game
shows and eating. She seldom ventured beyond
the mailbox of her parents' house. She wore the
same two outfits over and over. The first was a

pair of tight red pants that stretched so snugly over her backside Tommy feared they might pop like an over-inflated balloon. Her second outfit was a big, pink moo-moo that resembled a circus tent. Other times Penny wouldn't get dressed at all, and wandered about all day in blue pajamas. She had taken to checking the mailbox several times a day hoping for a letter from Lester.

Tommy was horrified one afternoon when she was checking the mailbox at the same time the school bus pulled up to drop him off. She was wearing her red pants that day, and the other students stared and snickered at Penny's sizable rump. The next day students were referring to him as "Tommy Buttle," which was shortened to "Buttle," and finally became "Butt-hole." There were two classmates who began bullying Tommy and instigating others to torment him. The larger of the boys was named Marty Malley. He was a year older than Tommy and had a protruding jaw, bucked teeth, and a flat-top haircut. Tommy thought he looked like a boy with the face of a horse. But worse than being ugly, Marty was a mean child who was quick to take advantage of anyone smaller or weaker than himself. His henchman was named Jimmy Smith, a small and nervous boy who frequently bore the brunt of Marty's cruelty, but nevertheless followed behind

Marty like a puppy. Tommy was beside himself with anger and humiliation about the name calling, but he didn't say or do anything. His response was to try to disappear. In his mind, his mother was responsible for all his problems. It was her fault they were stuck in Ohio, and her fault other boys were picking on him. No matter how Tommy tried to stay out of reach of Marty, he couldn't escape the older boy's cruel actions. His disappearing act didn't work.

One day in October, just after the start of the new school year, Tommy and Penny finally got their wishes. A large envelope arrived from Guatemala. There were three smaller envelopes inside the big one. One was a letter for Tommy, another for Penny, and the third contained legal papers for Penny to sign. Lester was asking for a divorce. Penny sat at the kitchen table looking stunned and yet more alert than Tommy had seen her since their arrival in Ohio. His grandmother sat next to her frowning and petting Penny's hand. His grandfather was across the table from them. He was wearing his spectacles, which gave him an air of authority, as he read the letter Lester had enclosed for Penny.

"It says here he is purchasing additional land. Wants to expand the mission's operation." Grandpa lifted his thick eyebrows and glanced over the top of his glasses at Penny, and then continued reading to himself. Penny's mouth opened and closed as she breathed, resembling a fish on dry land. She said nothing. Tommy watched her face turn red— almost red enough to match her pants.

Tommy picked up the large, empty envelope and looked at the stamps. Then he grabbed the letter with his name on it and went to his room. He closed the door behind him, and sat on the bed. The room's identity was gradually changing. Although the walls were still pink, his grandmother had put a Lone Ranger bedspread on the bed and there was a new lamp on the sewing-machine desk. Tommy felt uncertain. The letter he had waited so long for had finally arrived, but now he was afraid to open it. After a few moments of hesitation, Tommy ripped open the envelope and unfolded the letter. It said:

Dear Tommy,

I hope this letter finds you and Tammy well. I know Ohio must seem different to you, but it is a nice place to live. I am sorry I did not say goodbye before you left, but your mother wanted me gone and it seemed best under the circumstances. Please do not blame your mom because she could not stay. The mission life is hard and not everyone can make it. I have found a new partner to help in my work for the Lord. I cannot do it alone and I believe that God sent Lila to help me bear the burden now that you and your sister and mother are gone. But you will always be my son, and Tammy my daughter. I pray that God will look out for both of you and bring you happiness in your new life in the U.S. For the time being, you must grow up quickly, and watch out for your mom and sister. Lila and I will continue to do the Lord's work. We have purchased additional ground so we may expand our operation. We are starting a program to help poor children of Guatemala, not just in Canoguitas, but all of Guatemala. Please watch over Tammy, as she will need you. You are the man of the family now. You have always been a good boy and have made me proud. Maybe someday when you are older you can come back to Canoguitas for a visit.

Your loving father in Christ,
Lester J. Tuttle
Evangelical Friendship Mission of Guatemala

There was a five dollar bill enclosed along with a flier about the new program. It was a flier similar to those Tommy used to deliver on his bicycle throughout the town. It had faces drawn of little children with sad eyes and dark hair who stood with out-stretched hands. The caption read:

Evangelical Friendship Mission of Guatemala and The Tuttle House – A Safe Harbor In The Storm: A refuge for lost and abandoned children.

Tommy folded the letter, flier, and five-dollar bill and put them in the large envelope with the Guatemalan stamps. Then he folded the envelope in half and placed it in the bottom drawer of his dresser under his pants. He climbed on his bed and laid back on top of the Lone Ranger, his mind spinning with thoughts. *How,* Tommy wondered, *can I get to Tuttle House? Who are the kids on the flier? Are they riding my bicycle and playing with my bat?*

Tommy felt more confused than ever. His father hadn't answered any of the important questions Tommy had written about—questions like: *How is Molina? When can I come home?* What did his dad mean by "bear the burden?" Was he, Tommy, a burden? Didn't he try to help? Wasn't he always good with his Bible verses? Tommy was certain of one thing—he felt angry. He was angry with his mom, with his dad, and especially with this Lila person. Actually, he was angry with everyone— everyone except maybe Tammy.

It was quiet at the dinner table that night. The only conversation was about passing the potato chips or another hot dog please. Tommy noticed that his grandparents were watchful of his mother, and kept exchanging quick, worried glances. His mom ate remarkably little, which surprised Tommy because she so much loved potato chips. Everyone was eating but Penny, who only seemed to be playing with her food. By the end of the meal, only half of her hot dog was gone, and her plate was still full of chips and macaroni and cheese.

"Would you like some Spam, honey?" Grandma asked, but Penny just shook her head no.

Tommy got a second hot dog that night, and finished his mother's chips. After dinner, when the table was cleared and the dishes done, Grandma Mildred told Tommy and Tammy they could see whatever they wanted on television. They even told Tommy that he could change the channel. While Tommy and his sister watched a cowboy show, his grandparents were at the kitchen table, huddled with his mother, who had not moved since dinner. The conversation from the kitchen was steadily growing louder. Grandpa Joe was the only one Tommy could completely hear—probably because

Grandpa was hard of hearing and talked loudly. Unexpectedly, a fist hit the table, and he heard his grandfather curse for the first time.

"Someone sure as hell needs to tell them! Divorce! Adultery! They need to know just what kind of outfit they're supporting." Then Grandpa stood up and left the kitchen. A few minutes later he grabbed a jacket and fled from the house. The door slammed behind him. Tommy and Tammy were sent to bed.

The next evening there were special people coming to visit. The family ate early and Grandma made two batches of cookies—oatmeal and chocolate chip. Coffee was brewed and the small home was filled with delicious and inviting smells. Tommy couldn't wait for the company to arrive and hoped they wouldn't eat all the cookies. Grandma helped Penny get dressed in an outfit Tommy had never seen before. It was a navy blue dress with a white collar and a full skirt. She wore matching navy shoes that resembled ballerina slippers. Considering the bulk that loomed above, Tommy thought her feet looked remarkably small. She reminded him of the baby elephant's mother from *Dumbo*, a cartoon movie he had recently seen.

The company consisted of two men and a woman. They were serious-looking representatives from churches that contributed to the Evangelical

Friendship Mission of Guatemala. Once again the children were told to watch television while the adults sat in the dining room, located between the kitchen and living room. The dining room was only used for special events such as birthdays or holiday dinners. The last time they had used it was for Easter, several months earlier. Tonight there was a white tablecloth, and pieces of Grandma's white china. Six chairs were set around the table, and the adults were served coffee along with the cookies Grandma baked. Tammy and Tommy were given their own tray with cookies and two glasses of milk.

Grandpa did most of the talking at first. He sat at the head of the table with Grandma and Penny along one side. Grandma didn't say much, but Tommy saw her nod her head a lot. Penny spoke when asked a question, but her voice was too quiet for Tommy to hear. Penny looked uncomfortable in her navy dress. It emphasized her too-white skin. Her face was puffy and there were dark circles under her eyes. The company listened politely and nibbled cookies while Grandpa spoke. The mood at the table was somber. The letter that Lester had sent to Penny was passed around the table as the visitors took turns reading it. Tommy left the television set and crept close to the dining room where he could peek and hear better.

"So you can see what you're dealing with here," Grandpa said. "Lester is not a man entirely in control of his faculties." Grandma's hand rested beside his on the table, and he now cupped his hand over hers and leaned forward. "He's under some kind of spell. You know, voodoo or something similar. They practice stuff like that down there. *Brujeria* it's called, a kind of black magic. Penny's told us about some of it. The natives go to an *esperitista*—a person who deals with spirits, a kind of witch doctor. They might want a love potion or a mixture to put a spell on someone...or even kill a person. It's not as bad as what goes on in Haiti—there are no zombies to speak of—but it's the same sort of evil doing. The one thing I can assure you of is the devil has his hand in this."

No one spoke and Grandpa Joe continued, "This Lila woman Lester's taken up with—she's Guatemalan you know. She's a seductress. It sounds like she is now running the whole show. She's a looker, and from what I understand, a Jezebel and Delilah all rolled up into a single package. We thought you needed to know what's going on. You certainly can't continue to support this kind of operation."

Still no one responded, and the silence was increasingly uncomfortable.

"You do agree, don't you?" There was a

pleading quality to Grandpa's voice.

Finally one of the men cleared his throat and responded. "Mr. Ellis," he stated, looking at the plate of cookies in the center of the table, "this is an extremely awkward situation. I can imagine how upset you must be, and let me express my deepest sympathies to your daughter." He stopped and cleared his throat again. "We have heard from Brother Lester regarding this matter, and he is also concerned about your daughter. It seems she has had difficulty adapting to missionary life."

"She's had difficulty adapting to a philandering husband—that's where the difficulty is!" Grandpa Joe protested.

The man quickly raised his hand and shook his head. "Please, Mr. Ellis. We are not here to upset you. We share your concern, but we must be honest if we are to be of help. We have received letters and reports from Brother Lester documenting the difficulties of life in the field. It is no reflection on Penny here. Most American women would not be able to stand the test: the language differences, sickness, the demands of raising young children, and the harsh living conditions. For years Lester has expressed reservations about Penny and her resolve to remain in Guatemala. Yet, despite these concerns Lester has succeeded in managing the mission and spreading the Gospel. Through his efforts, with the help of God, our program in Guatemala is thriving! Isn't this what it's really about? What these two fine people set out to do? Of course rejection is never pleasant, but let's keep our perspective here."

Grandpa just stared at the speaker, not even attempting to respond. He looked deflated. Penny remained silent and pale faced.

The man continued, "As you know, God moves in mysterious ways. Sometimes His plans are different from our own. Although it may not seem fair, there are times when sacrifices are needed. It seems God frequently makes the greatest demands on those He loves the most. We must remember it's the mission that counts; not the personal happiness of any two individuals. Lester and Penny are being asked to make a sacrifice. It's obvious, I think, they are truly favored by God."

Grandpa suddenly erupted, "That's fine for you to say! You aren't the ones being asked to make a sacrifice, are you? It's my daughter and grandchildren who are making the sacrifice. Not to mention the sacrifice my wife, Mildred, and I are making. We are expected to just sit here and watch? He's a felon, for goodness sake."

Grandpa was abruptly interrupted, this time by the second man who had not spoken until now. "I respectfully remind you that Brother Lester has paid his debt to society. I would also remind you what the Bible says about forgiveness. Nevertheless we are prepared to make a generous offer to your daughter on behalf of the mission. We try to take care of our own." The new man spoke with authority and a deep voice. He appeared the older of the men, with gray hair and wrinkles around his eyes. He was dressed the most casually, in a white shirt with a beige sweater and khaki pants. "The divorce is for the benefit of the children, your daughter, and the mission. It is a sacrifice that Brother Lester has reluctantly agreed to, with the stipulation that arrangements be made to help Penny. That is why he is generously offering to pay for her half of the property. In addition, during her time of transition, it only seems fair that a portion of the mission funds be allotted to Penny and the children, as an acknowledgement of her past contribution to this worthwhile project. And…" he paused for a second and then continued, "for the record, Brother Lester denies an affair."

Grandpa was exasperated. "You're buying her off?" He glared at the men. "You don't care what's going on down there so long as you have a successful mission program to brag about! You're all so smug in your righteousness. It's the devil working here and you don't have the sense to see it!"

The beige-sweater man shook his head. "Please, Mr. Ellis, calm down. Think of your daughter and what she's already been through."

As if on cue, Penny began to shudder and tears burst from her eyes. She was a giant dam that could no longer hold back the water. Once again she began to wail, as she had seven months earlier in Guatemala. The eerie sound startled those at the table and they turned to her with eyes wide in surprise. For Tommy, the wail was unbearable and animal-like; it matched a chord deep within him where he had a similar but silent wail for all he had lost. Upon hearing her, Tammy immediately began to cry. Tommy returned to the couch in the living room and tried to comfort his sister, while Grandma Mildred wrapped her arms around Penny. The guests were standing now, and over the commotion some papers were put in Grandpa's hands.

"Take some time, Mr. Ellis; don't be hasty. Think of your daughter and grandchildren. Please let us help."

Then the visitors left. Grandma and Grandpa led Penny to her bedroom, and Tammy followed after them. Tommy was alone in the living room. He turned off the television and listened. The sobbing continued at a more subdued level, and he imagined it might go on for some time. It had been a long day and there was a lot to think about. He took the tray and empty glasses into the kitchen. Then he came back to the dining room table and grabbed a handful of cookies. Tommy went into his room and quietly closed the door behind him. He kicked off his shoes and got into bed. That night he ate cookies in the dark and thought about Canoguitas. He searched every memory—each face, and hut, and road he could recall before he finally fell asleep. Then in his dreams he continued to search. He was searching for his dad in Canoguitas. He was searching for the Devil. When he found him, he was sitting at a table playing cards with a serpent that had arms and hands and a beautiful face. Tommy picked up a stick and began to beat his father. The snake-woman kept writhing and told Tommy to hit him again.

****

The following afternoon Tommy was riding his bicycle in circles around an entrance to the city park. It was Saturday, and he had spent the morning doing chores. A plan had come to him in the night and he got up early to make preparations. It felt good to finally be doing something about his problems, rather than just waiting like his mother did and feeling sorry for himself.

He rode his bike in slow circles making

figure eights and waiting to see what would happen. It was a quiet afternoon. The temperature was nice but there was a gusty wind. This side of the park was deserted, and Tommy watched the empty swings move in the wind as if being pushed by ghosts. He was about to give up and go home for the day when he noticed two bicycles heading toward him. He turned toward the riders and stopped to get a better look. It was Marty Malley and Jimmy Smith. The horse-faced boy and his little buddy would surely take the bait. When he was certain, Tommy slowly turned his bike around and headed toward home. He peddled a short way before looking back, and confirmed they were following him and closing in fast—just as he had planned.

"Hey Butt-hole," one yelled. "Wanna run? What's the matter? Ya scared?" Tommy pumped his bike faster, heading toward a large oak tree he knew was just around the curve. He felt his hands perspire on the handlebars as he heard the laughter and taunts behind him. But he was prepared. When Tommy reached the oak tree, he pretended that his bicycle had lost traction, and it looked like he had fallen on the ground. This delighted his tormentors who quickly caught up with him. They jumped off their bikes and ran toward him.

Marty arrived first and reached to grab the back of Tommy's shirt. That was a mistake. Tommy turned, smiling broadly and Marty looked at him with a curious expression until he felt the bat smash against his shoulder. The baseball bat hit with such force that Marty, the horse-faced boy, was thrown off balance and flew sideways, landing at Jimmy's feet. As Marty rolled on the gravel grabbing his arm, Jimmy stood transfixed with a look of disbelief on his face. Too late it registered that Tommy was headed straight toward him. Jimmy turned to run but the bat caught his thigh and he tumbled down beside Marty screaming in agony. Both boys were now on the ground scurrying like crabs across a beach toward the bikes they had left by the side of the road. But Tommy darted ahead and beat them to their bikes. He stood with the bat pointing at them shouting in Spanish. The boys sat motionless and Marty began to whimper, trying hard not to cry, but failing in his effort. "Tommy, please," he sobbed. "We're done here. Please let us go."

Jimmy started to get to his feet, but Tommy whammed the bat down on the ground, inches from his foot, and Jimmy fell back again. "Come on, man," he whined. "We're sorry. Aren't we Marty? We won't bother you any more. We promise."

Tommy looked down at the two boys with contempt. He hadn't planned what to do next, but it all just rolled off his tongue without his ever having thought about it. He began his tirade with the word *"cerotes" (bastards)*, a word he would never have been permitted to say when he lived in Guatemala. He spoke Spanish and English, mixing the languages together.

Marty and Jimmy looked at one another and then at Tommy, who was now taking the bat to their bicycles, as if punctuating each phrase with a dent in the metal.

"A curse on you!" Tommy screamed. "A curse I learned in Guatemala from the most powerful bruja-wizard in the jungle. You'll crap frogs and pee like a girl if you bother me again. Understand? Your parents will disappear and you will fail at everything you do for the rest of your lives." Tommy paused to let this sink in. "And, if you ever call me Butt-hole again, you'll wish you were never born." He raised the bat above his head and glared at Marty and Jimmy.

Marty rocked and moaned, clutching his shoulder, clearly in pain.

"Now swear to me," Tommy said. *"Jurame."*

Both boys nodded in unison. "I swear," they each said.

"I swear not to bother you or to call you… you know, that word," Jimmy replied.

Marty nodded in agreement. Tears were streaming down his cheeks. "Me too," he whimpered.

"You've been warned," Tommy said, lowering the bat. "Whatever happens to you now is your fault, not mine. If you break your oath you will be cursed, and I know what I'm talking about. I've seen what a curse can do." He went to his bicycle as Marty and Jimmy slowly rose to their feet.

"Buenos días," Tommy said, putting his right foot on the pedal of his bike.

Tommy was never called Buttle or Butt-hole again.

6
ADOPTED

I can't recall a time when the concept of adoption wasn't part of my world. This probably had a lot to do with the fact that I looked different from my parents and other people where I grew up in Michigan. There are a lot of fair-haired, pale-skinned people here—descendants of the Vikings and the offspring of Scandinavian immigrants. And these are tall people. My dark hair and deep olive skin stand out a lot. And I am small; only about five feet tall. I more closely resemble the Chippewa Indians who live in our county and operate the casino. But in Michigan, even the Indians are big. I remember my father telling me that when he first moved here and heard there was an Indian reservation, he half-expected to find people riding horses and living in tepees. Of course that's not what he found. Instead, he found people driving new cars and living in fine homes.

As a child, I became used to people—total strangers—asking where I was from. My mom would be pushing me in a shopping cart through K-Mart, and some smiling, pink-cheeked stranger would approach us and announce, "She's not from here, is she? Where did you get her?" It was as if I was an item that might be found on isle six or perhaps as a Blue-Light Special.

Mia tried to be polite, and used such occasions as an opportunity to educate people. "This is my daughter," she'd reply. "I adopted her from Guatemala."

Someone else might observe, "She sure doesn't look like you."

To this, Mia would say, "You're right. My daughter is far prettier than me or her father, thank goodness."

My mom always saw the best in people and forgave these intrusions into our private world because, as she put it, "They don't mean anything by it. They're just curious because you are so pretty and unique looking." However, my dad would have none of it. He made a game of thinking up ridiculous responses to the inquiries. When a person asked where I was from he loved to respond by saying I was from Ireland or Sweden. Once, when someone noted I didn't look like either of my parents, he agreed and informed them that I looked like his first wife, who was an Eskimo and had ventured to Lapland to pursue her dream of racing reindeer.

I always knew I was adopted because there was no way the world would not let me know. At home, Daniel and Mia spoke of my adoption with reverence. They even made a life book—the story of how we became a family. The book began with pictures of the two of them meeting in Israel, followed by their wedding on a cruise ship in New York. Then it jumps to the farm in Michigan that has been my home for as long as I can remember. The story goes that it was lonely on the farm, with only the two of them and some cats and livestock. Then I came, first in pictures and finally for real. There are pictures of me in Guatemala right after I was born and then more photos of me and Mom together when she stayed in Guatemala during the adoption. Grace and Tommy are in some of the photographs along with people I don't know and some peacocks. The book ends with a snapshot of me home with my mom and dad, my adoption complete and the three of us together. That's how our family was born. I still have my life book and enjoy looking at it to this day.

One thing I can tell you about adoption is that in some ways it makes life a little simpler, at least it did for me. If you want to be rebellious, adoption gives you something to get fired up about—a cause to throw yourself into. And you know that incomplete feeling that we all get sometimes? If you're adopted, you think you know the reason for that feeling. Even though you're probably wrong, it'll take a long time to figure it out, and by then it won't really matter any more. Because by then you'll realize everyone has that feeling sometimes, adopted or not. When it gets right down to it, life is a puzzle we each have to solve on our own, like a personal Rubik's Cube. But when you're adopted, your puzzle is right there in front of you, like a big silent mountain just waiting to be climbed. And if you're lucky, like me, you have a book of magic spells to help guide you along the way.

7
FROZEN

Lester's divorce from Penny was eventually granted. He kept his word and sent Penny payment for the land they had owned together. Then for a year, she received a check every month from the Evangelical Friendship Mission of Guatemala. Penny's mother, who was a talented seamstress, began to share her skills with her daughter, teaching Penny how to alter and repair clothes. Penny worked at home, hemming slacks and making repairs for a local dry cleaner and various clothing stores. When she had proved herself to be both quick and capable, other assignments came her way, and through word-of-mouth she developed a following of regular customers. By the time Tammy was seven years old, she, too, was part of the sewing team. Tammy could hem as well as any adult.

Grandma's seldom-used dining room became the sewing shop, which was now full of projects. On his thirteenth birthday, Tommy received a new bicycle, and he rode it downtown to the clothing stores doing pick-ups and deliveries for his mother. Penny paid him for his help, which gave him status with his classmates. His family struggled economically, but he always had more change in his pocket than the other kids.

Tommy still thought about Guatemala, but he was getting used to life in Ohio. He regarded childhood as something he would just have to endure. Once he was an adult, he could get on with his real life.

Now that Mom was busy, she almost seemed happy. She had taken in an orange cat that she named Marsh, and she talked to him all the time— just as if he was a person. She would even apologize to Marsh if she accidentally stepped on his tail or had to move him from her spot on the couch. She was eating less and had started walking on a regular basis. She lost about sixty pounds. Penny was still a big woman, but now she was not so large that men ignored her completely. Mr. O'Brien, who owned a men's clothing shop, often quizzed Tommy about his mother whenever Tommy came by for Penny's deliveries.

"How is your mom?" he would ask as he dabbed his forehead with a white handkerchief. "She works too hard. She should get out and have some fun."

Tommy would shrug, "She's okay."

Mr. O'Brien was a heavy-set man who wore suspenders. He was balding, and his round face was usually flushed and damp with perspiration. Tommy didn't want to encourage Mr. O'Brien's interest in his mother. One fat person in the family was enough. He could imagine the jokes that a pairing of his mother and Mr. O'Brien might inspire. That thought had kept him awake on more than one night as he remembered his episode with the two bullies, Marty and Jimmy. Tommy had made a place for himself at school, and he didn't want Mr. O'Brien or his mother messing it up.

Aside from the fact that Mr. O'Brien was overweight, Tommy had another reason for not wanting him or any other man going out with his mother. Divorce was a rarity in his small Ohio town, and even though it was considered shameful, Tommy could tell that others were intrigued by his story. Whenever Tommy talked of his mother or life in Guatemala, he would embellish and exaggerate the events, telling about witches, devils, and magic spells, and how he and his sister and mother had fled Guatemala in fear for their lives.

"You don't mess around once a curse is put on you. You get the hell out of there or you die. And that's what we did—we got out."

Few of his friends completely believed the stories, but they liked hearing him tell them. Tommy feared that if his mother ever married someone like Mr. O'Brien, the very essence of ordinary, his stories would go from interesting to boring and become a joke.

Other than Grandpa Joe, Tommy felt uncomfortable around men. He found them more difficult to deal with than women, who were usually friendly. Women smiled at him and often commented on his blue eyes. One woman for whom Penny sewed had called his eyes "mesmerizing." Tommy checked the dictionary. He didn't completely understand the definition, but knew it was a compliment.

Most of Tommy's teachers were women, so even when he got into trouble at school he was quickly forgiven. "It's understandable," they would say to his mother and grandparents. "After all, Tommy has special circumstances. Consider all he's been through: being a refugee, fleeing a foreign country, suffering through a divorce. A certain amount of mischief is to be expected."

****

One night when Tommy was fifteen years old, he came home from a football game and found Mr. O'Brien and Penny sitting on the couch with Marsh the cat between them.

They both stood up awkwardly when Tommy came in. "Tommy, you know Mr. O'Brien," Penny beamed. "Pat, this is my son, Tommy."

They shook hands formally, as if meeting for

the first time. Mr. O'Brien, whose face and head were red as a tomato, said, "Please call me Pat."

Tommy nodded and said, "Hello, Pat." He sensed immediately that Mr. O'Brien was not comfortable being on a first-name basis with a kid. Tommy was not surprised. *Adults always say things they don't really mean.*

His mother smiled. "Pat owns Patrick's Men's Shop. You know, the clothing and haberdashery store."

Tommy nodded, "Yeah, Mom. I make deliveries there all the time."

"Thomas and I know each other well," Pat said, grinning. "We're old friends."

Tommy winced. *Liar,* he thought. *We're not friends, new or old. And don't call me Thomas.* But he kept his voice and expression indifferent. "Where is everyone?" Tommy asked. His grandparents seldom went out at night during the week.

"Oh, Grandma and Grandpa took Tammy for ice cream. Pat and I had some business to discuss." Pat and Penny both grinned.

Another lie, Tommy thought. *Unless you're talking about monkey business.*

"Well," Pat said, "it's getting late and I should get home. I don't want to keep Penny from her beauty sleep." He patted Marsh on the head, and Penny walked with him to the front door. She got Pat's coat from the closet and watched as he buttoned up.

Tommy left for his bedroom so he wouldn't have to be there if they decided to get mushy. *Beauty sleep? Is he crazy?*

"Nice seeing you again, Thomas," Pat said loudly as Tommy left the room.

"You, too, but my name is Tommy." He closed his bedroom door, already trying to figure out how to thwart this romance.

Pat was determined and he soon became a regular guest. Tommy learned that Pat was a widower, with nine-year-old twins named Melody and Victoria. Mrs. O'Brien had died from a brain embolism several years earlier, and Pat's parents, who lived in a house up the street, helped care for the girls. All the family seemed happy with Pat's attention to Penny except Tommy. Given Mr. O'Brien's frequent visits, Tommy wasn't surprised when, shortly after his sixteenth birthday, Penny and Patrick decided to marry.

He was in his bedroom when Penny broke the news. Tommy sat on the edge of the bed, feeling heavy with resignation.

Penny was in the chair by his desk. "There is going to be a transition," she said. "Pat says we should take it one step at a time. Besides, we'll need to sell his house and buy a bigger one before there will be room for all of us."

"There's not enough room at Pat's house?" Tommy asked skeptically. He had ridden by Mr. O'Brien's home on his bicycle, and he could clearly picture it in his mind, a two-story colonial house surrounded by a large well-manicured yard.

"No. Not yet. But there will be." Penny paused, looking at Tommy. "In the meantime, Grandma and Grandpa will love having you here. You're such a help to them."

Tommy listened quietly, hurt by her words even though he didn't really like Pat or his daughters. He knew that the story about selling the house was probably a lie, a cover-up. Hearing her words, Tommy felt his world growing smaller and emptier. He had lost Canoguitas, his dad, and the life he loved in Guatemala. His life in Ohio was far from ideal, but now even that was being chipped away. While his mother and Tammy "got settled" in their new home with Patrick, Tommy would stay with his grandparents. Soon nothing would be left—just an empty world, as cold and lifeless as Antarctica. Tommy would be little more than a ghost or bystander stranded in a frozen wasteland, while others had a place in the real world. He could have cried, but his tears were like everything else in Antarctica—frozen.

"You'll be just fine," Penny said softly,

looking at the still-pink walls as if noticing their color for the first time.

"I know," Tommy answered. *I'm always fine,* he thought.

"Oh, Tommy," Penny sighed. She walked over to the bed and sat beside him, causing the bed to creak. He was heaved against her in the big bowl in the mattress caused by their weight. Penny hugged him. "We've been through a lot together, and I know it's been hard. But believe me, it will be better now. I promise. And guess what!" she hugged him even tighter, "I have a surprise for you. It was Pat's idea. He thought now that you're old enough, you might like a car!"

Tommy could hardly believe his ears. He pulled away from his mother's embrace and stared at her.

Penny nodded her head and grinned at him. "Yes, a car! Pat thought you'd need it for school and all the sports you're involved with. Otherwise, you'll wear poor Grandpa out, driving you back and forth. But don't say a word. It's a secret until the wedding."

Suddenly there was a little sunshine in Antarctica. A car of his own was more than Tommy could have hoped for out of this marriage, but it also exposed the lie. It appeared he would be staying with Grandma and Grandpa for a long,

long time.

****

As soon as Penny and Patrick returned from their honeymoon in Florida, Tommy received his car, a red Chevy Corvair that was almost new. While the movers were taking Tammy and Penny's belongings to the new house, Tommy drove around town taking friends for an after-school ride in his car. He discovered he had more friends than he realized.

Once Penny and Tammy were out of the house, Grandma told Tommy he could switch rooms and take the larger bedroom, but he declined the offer. He was fine where he was, and he liked the pink walls, which were really ugly and seemed appropriate for his situation. Marsh the cat was also left behind, and soon became a fixture at the foot of Tommy's bed. Sometimes Tommy found himself talking to Marsh as his mother had done.

Just as Tommy suspected, the O'Brien house never went up for sale. He often drove by there with friends, who would exclaim how lucky he was to have Mr. O'Brien as a stepfather. He heard how fortunate he was to have his own car, to live independently (practically) with his grandparents, to get an allowance, and to have free clothes from

Patrick's Men's Shop. *It is amazing how stupid people can be.* Tommy saw all his privileges as little more than bribes. He enjoyed the payoff, but often wondered what was so awful about him that his family didn't want him around. He didn't know why, but he knew he'd somehow lost out. Even Tammy acted differently, as if he was a stranger. The twins doted on Tammy, and the three girls had become inseparable. Whenever he stopped by to take Tammy for a ride, she was either at a ballet lesson or practicing the piano. Tommy watched helplessly from his iceberg as Tammy and his mother slowly drifted away. He wondered how long it would be before his grandparents floated away, too.

The only place Tommy felt appreciated was at school, where he excelled at sports, especially soccer. Although he was one of the best players, neither his parents nor grandparents came to his games. He didn't boast of his accomplishments to his family, and they were always too busy to ask. He revealed little of himself to his friends, certain that if he said too much, they would see the "true" Tommy—the "unacceptable" Tommy—and he would lose them as well.

Tommy's secretiveness increased his popularity with the girls. He was mysteriously silent, and that, along with his good looks, gave him a certain charisma. The girls he dated would start by asking him questions—which he skillfully dodged—and end up talking about themselves and their feelings for the better part of their dates. They would sit in the dark in his car and jabber away about something their girlfriend said that made them angry, and how their parents were too old-fashioned to understand their problems, or how they wanted to be an artist someday and travel to France. Tommy would patiently listen, amazed at how much of nothing a girl could talk about, and occasionally he'd interject a question or a sigh. Eventually, he would start playing with her hair while she chattered. Then gradually he would start rubbing her shoulders. Finally she would look at him and tell him how beautiful his eyes were. "Your eyes are...so blue, so sad, so...," blah...blah...blah.

He liked his eyes, too. They served him well. He would gaze at the girl beside him, and his eyes would cast a spell—the spell she so much wanted to be under. By the time his hands were unfastening her brassiere, he would hear, "Do you love me? Tell me you love me."

The first time he heard that question, he wasn't sure how to reply. *What does it matter? Say anything. Say what she wants to hear.*

"I don't know," he would reply with dramatic resignation. He'd pull his hand away and look longingly into the girl's face. "I'm not sure I know what love is. I do know that you're beautiful, and I've never in my life felt this way before." That was usually enough. Amazingly, his partner capitulated by taking his hand and placing it over her breast. Tommy liked the challenge. If the truth didn't work then he would invent his own truth to manipulate the reluctant young woman. There was a place for lying and it was, after all, a family tradition. His father had lied to get him out of Guatemala and now Pat and his mother lied to get what they wanted. They were all liars. Why should he be different? Lying is what adults do. He was the same as them. But if he was going to be a liar he was going to be the best, most convincing liar he could. With a few well-chosen words spoken at the right time, he scored and his frozen loneliness temporarily melted.

Unlike his family, girls appreciated him. Aside from his eyes, they liked his dark, wavy hair and athletic build. They loved his soothing voice and the Spanish words he sometimes whispered in their ear during lovemaking. "Querida. Mi amour..." They appreciated how he clung to them afterward and held them close, never rushing to get up and be on his way. He knew all this because they told him. They trusted him because "he was sincere."

In his senior year, Tommy was captain of the football team. He had slept with several cheerleaders and other popular girls who had caught his eye. By now the words he used for seduction were like a script; he was an actor who played a part well. Tommy was invited to parties and considered a good guy to have around. Besides, he could keep a secret. Even his mother and stepfather began reaching out to him, inviting him to dinner and family events. Pat was adopting Tammy and wanted to adopt Tommy, if he was willing.

The adoption seemed important to his mother, but Tommy considered it meaningless. "I'm already grown," he said. "What's the point?"

He awoke one Saturday morning to find Penny sitting at the end of the bed, holding Marsh. "Tommy," she said. "Please do this. Do it for yourself as much as for me. The adoption may not seem like much, but it can open doors. It's an acknowledgment of Pat's feelings for you. Pat's an important man in this community. He's a civic leader and he belongs to Rotary."

Tommy was intrigued, even though it seemed like no big deal. What doors could possibly open by being adopted by Pat O'Brien, haberdasher? He couldn't think of any, but he reasoned it couldn't hurt. Who knows? There might be some future benefit.

"Fine," he said. "But I'm not changing my name."

"That's all right," Penny answered. "You don't have to change your name now or ever. You can always change it later if you want."

So Pat and Tommy went through with the adoption, and afterward Pat hung a picture of Tommy taken at a soccer game (which Pat had not actually attended) on one wall of his store. The caption beneath the picture read "Favorite Son." *More like only son,* Tommy thought, *and not quite that—just another lie.*

The store was now attracting a younger clientele, and Tommy wondered if his adoption by Pat had simply been a ruse to drum up business. To Tommy, that seemed as likely an explanation as any.

During the Christmas holidays, Pat and Penny questioned Tommy about his future after high school. "What about college?" they asked. Pat suggested applying for an athletic scholarship, adding that he would be willing to pay Tommy's tuition if he chose an in-state college.

"What do you want to do?" Penny asked, with a sense of urgency.

"I'm not sure," Tommy said truthfully. "I'm studying the matter."

He was considering what he should do, but

he wasn't ready to share the plan that came more clearly into focus with each passing day: before he did anything else, he wanted to revisit the kingdom he had lost eight years earlier. He needed to see Canoguitas again with his own eyes.

Would it be as he remembered it, or were even his own memories lies? And what of the father who had banished him—the ex-con turned man-of-God? Was Lester what he claimed to be, or just another pitchman? Tommy still had the letter his father had sent him before the divorce. Every now and then, he would take it out to read it and look at the five dollar bill he had never spent. The desertion no longer made him angry; instead, he was filled with a profound sense of emptiness. Tommy now knew what really happened that night so long ago when he witnessed his mother's anguish. Apparently, Lester had become romantically involved with a young Guatemalan woman named Lila. That fateful night in the clinic, his mother had confronted Lester and given him an ultimatum: Lester must choose between Penny and the kids or Lila. Lester chose Lila. Now, years later, Tommy wanted—needed—to know why. What made Lila so special that a man would walk out on his family? Leaving a wife maybe Tommy could understand. But leaving children? No. Tommy could not comprehend how a man could do that.

Were he and his sister so unimportant? What was so special about Guatemala? Why did he want to return? Was it his father, his memories, or perhaps his future?

Penny and Pat listened quietly when Tommy finally shared his plan with them, their stiff postures revealing their discomfort with his idea. Outside it was snowing, but Pat kept dabbing at the perspiration on his face and neck.

"How do you know he'll even want you there?" asked Pat. "Have you written him yet?"

"No," Tommy replied. "I don't know if he'll want me to come or not. But that doesn't matter. I need to go there for myself. If he doesn't want to see me, okay. I don't need his permission to travel to Guatemala."

"Well, of course not, but shouldn't you at least let him know you're coming?" Pat persisted. "That would be the considerate thing to do."

Penny said nothing, watching Tommy with a worried expression.

Tommy shrugged. "Okay, I'll tell you what, Pat. You let him know. It's a little late for me to start corresponding again. He doesn't answer my letters, anyway. I've only gotten one letter in eight years. He's never been considerate of me, so why should I care? I just want to see the country. If you guys think being considerate is so important, then you let him know."

Tommy had hoped to catch Lester unaware, without time to run away and start lying again. He didn't like the idea of writing ahead of time. He wanted to just show up and ask how his chicken, Molina, was doing. If he inconvenienced his convict-turned-preacher father, so much the better.

"But what about college?" Penny asked. "You could major in Spanish and become a teacher. They make a good living."

"I've sent off for some applications. I'm giving it a lot of thought. Who knows? We'll see what happens. I'm not in a hurry."

"How far have you gotten with your travel plans so far?" asked Pat.

"I've saved three hundred dollars for my trip. I could use a little help with the ticket and passport. I can work for you in the store to earn more money." Tommy was quite confident Pat didn't want him around. The picture on the wall was enough.

Pat glanced at Penny, who simply nodded. "That won't be necessary," Pat said. "You do have a graduation coming up, and we planned to give you a present. Something special. I suppose if this trip helps you find yourself, it's a good investment."

"Pat, I'm not trying to find myself. I'm trying to find my chicken. Besides, I'm not lost. I'm still a Tuttle and I want to see Tuttle House. And, I'd like to be a tourist and go sightseeing. What better place to go than the place where I started out? Or better yet, where I was kicked out? But thank you, Pat. I appreciate any help you and Mom can give."

As he left for home that night, Tommy wondered why he didn't like his stepfather more. Pat had always been good to him and had mostly kept his word. Pat was a decent man—better than his other father. Still, Tommy had always resented Pat from the day he first met him.

****

Five months later, a week after his graduation from high school, Tommy received his new passport, along with a ticket to Guatemala with the return date left open.

The next week he packed for his trip. The first suitcase was full and closed. The second was lying open on his bed. Before snapping it shut, he pulled the old envelope from Guatemala out of his dresser drawer and tucked it inside. Marsh watched from the foot of the bed. "Sorry, cat," Tommy said, rubbing the top of Marsh's head. Marsh looked up and started to purr.

Tommy grabbed a suitcase in each hand and looked around at the pink walls one final time before leaving. "What an ugly room," he said. "Well, its all yours now, Marsh. I hope you like pink." Tommy turned and left the room.

Jim & Cheryl Pahz

8
RELIGION

Tommy and my father, Daniel, are two completely different men who somehow both wound up at Theophilus College and both fell in love with the same girl. Religion brought them to the point where their paths crossed, but each approached religion in a different way. It would be hard to separate Tommy from religion. I don't believe he realized it was the essential medium that supported his being, in the way that soil is the medium that supports a plant. Religion was elemental and always there, his to be taken and used as he desired—kind of like a raincoat. If it was raining outside, he would wear his raincoat; when the weather was nice, he left it home. But the raincoat was there for him, waiting in his closet if he needed it. Tommy never stopped to wonder where the raincoat had come from or if he was worthy of wearing it. But at least Tommy knew where he belonged and never doubted it. At Theophilus College, he thrived, even if it was for the wrong reasons.

With my father, religion was a different matter entirely. Religion was never taken for granted because it was never easy for him, and he pondered it all the time. If he was a Christian, he worried about disappointing his father. If he accepted Judaism, might it not be a betrayal of his mother? That's not even taking into account the really big questions like which religion is right, or in which house of worship God belongs. Guilt was the medium in which my father grew; guilt and uncertainty. He described his situation to me as his interfaith dilemma which he defined as "almost chosen, nearly saved, always troubled. That's what happens," he said, "when you're born into different religions. You don't know where you belong."

My dad's struggle with religion began when he was ten years old. While Tommy was being booted out of Guatemala by his father and shipped off to Ohio, Daniel Fisher attended Woodlawn Academy, an Episcopalian school on Long Island, New York. The fact that a Jewish father and Baptist mother didn't foresee a problem with their son attending a private Christian academy is a testament to the gentle and trusting nature of my grandparents.

At Woodlawn, Daniel had his first encounter with anti-Semitism. Right before Easter his teacher asked him in front of the class if he was Jewish, and if he would recite some of those "funny Hebrew chants." He answered he didn't know any chants and didn't speak Hebrew. He also said his family practiced tolerance. That was the moment my dad realized he didn't know to which religion he belonged. To this day, my dad talks about his encounter with Mrs. Odykirk. She was his elementary school teacher and his first anti-Semite, and she came to represent to him everything in the world that is evil. Dad says that incident with his teacher was the first domino that started knocking over all the other dominos of his religious life. One thing led to another. And although he had a satisfactory answer for Mrs. Odykirk, he wasn't sure what "tolerance" meant, and had to ask my grandmother when he got home from school that day.

Uncertainty was awakened and questions were revealed that eventually led my dad to the evangelical college in Tennessee where he met Grace and Tommy. The name of the school was Theophilus College, and the word Theophilus comes from Greek meaning "friend of God." Dad told me he had been worried about his brain because he couldn't remember ever applying to this school, and then years later he discovered that his mother had applied for him. Nevertheless, he was grateful to be accepted to Theophilus. He said it was the sixties and he had been doing drugs, so the fact that he didn't remember applying didn't seem that remarkable. He loved Theophilus, although at first he hated it. He still talks about his school days at Theophilus with affection. His yearbook is a prized possession. After Theophilus, his search for enlightenment took him to Israel where he found Mia, my mother.

A stupid question posed to a ten-year-old boy in a grade school classroom was an instrument of fate. What happened in that classroom was so powerful it hurled my father on a collision course with my mom. But something else happened in that room on that day, something wonderful. That was the day my father first said my name out loud. On that day he gave his oral report on the quetzal bird of Guatemala. He could have chosen any bird he wanted for his presentation, but the quetzal was the only one he was interested in. Why? He told me when the quetzal looked out at him from the pages of the *National Geographic Magazine*, it called to him. It was as if he recognized it. Maybe it was me, his daughter, he recognized even though I was yet to be born. A path was being laid.

Fate and destiny are all around us, unfolding in mysterious ways. For Tommy, religion was a tool to be used. For Daniel, it was a riddle to be solved. For me, it is a miracle to be celebrated. I do this by creating alters. My mother taught me the art of mosaics and creating images and worlds using found objects. I create my alters by bringing together small, unrelated items in absurd and sometimes beautiful ways. I don't really think about or plan my alters. I just respond to what moves me at the time. And when I'm finished I wait to see what happens. Sometimes I give the alter away. Sometimes I set it in an unexpected place, like the blue and green egg alter at the front of my chicken coop. Usually I place it in my display area at the Mountain Town Gallery (where I sell my work), and wait for it to be found. It might take a while, but eventually someone buys it and takes it home. The right person always comes along.

Jim & Cheryl Pahz

9
THE MISSION

After clearing customs, Tommy walked through a gate into the arrival area of the Guatemala International Airport. A small crowd of people was waiting on the other side of the barrier. An attractive young woman with short-cropped, reddish-brown hair held up a piece of poster board with his name written on it—Tommy Tuttle. She wore blue jeans with a white T-shirt and looked to be about his age.

"Hi," Tommy said, walking up to her. "I'm Tommy."

"JoAnn," she replied, offering a pleasant smile.

Tommy was surprised. He had expected to be met at the airport by either his father or one of the Guatemalan parishioners. JoAnn was obviously North American.

As if reading Tommy's mind, JoAnn stated, "I'm doing my field training by working with the ministry. This way I can assist Brother Lester and get college credit."

"Field training?" Tommy was puzzled. "What's that?"

"I'm a student at Theophilus College. It's a Christian school in Nashville. Before graduating, students take time off from studying to have a practical experience. It's called field training; sort of like volunteer work. Actually, it is volunteer work, only we pay for the privilege of doing it and get college credit. Some students go to missions, some work in inner cities, and a few help plant new churches. My work is with the Evangelical Friendship Mission of Guatemala—your father's program."

JoAnn tossed the sign in a wire wastebasket. "Okay," she said. "Let's get your luggage. I have a car waiting outside."

They continued talking as they picked up Tommy's baggage and left the airport terminal. As soon as they exited the building, Tommy was surrounded by children begging for money. *"No tenemos nada,"* JoAnn said tersely to the beggars. Tommy noticed the acrid smell in the air, a mixture of grime and exhaust fumes. The pollution was so thick he felt it cling to his skin. He didn't recall this strong smell of petroleum from his childhood memories. He followed JoAnn to where the car and driver were waiting, and JoAnn introduced the driver whose name was Juan. Juan was a short man with a front tooth missing from his smile. Nevertheless, Juan grinned broadly and greeted Tommy with enthusiasm. *"Mucho traffico,"* Juan said. Then in broken English, "We leave now, perhaps?"

The drive to the province of Esquintla took three hours and Tommy found the trip exciting. First, there was the traffic and congestion of the city. There seemed to be few driving rules; busses flew by while people on bicycles and motorcycles recklessly wove in and out of traffic. Driving was an interactive sport in the city, accompanied by much horn honking, shouting, and cursing. Tommy noticed the majority of vehicles were old trucks and cars dating back fifteen to twenty years. One Plymouth was a model from the early 1950's. Everybody seemed to be in a hurry.

Once the congestion was behind them, the smell of the city diminished, and villages and countryside offered colorful and panoramic views. This was more like Tommy remembered: vivid greens against a blue sky; pink and yellow stucco houses like popsicles; a tiny shack by the side of the road where an Indian woman sold flowers and rice milk. Tommy sat quietly absorbing the sights and sounds that his body seemed thirsty for. He was comforted by the occasional Spanish word or phrase that drifted by as the car moved through villages further away from the city. They were heading toward the coastal jungle and more Mayan Indians appeared along the roadside, dressed in traditional, hand-woven skirts and embroidered tops.

After an hour into the trip, Juan stopped the car to buy gas and get drinks. The temperature was warmer as they passed from a temperate climate zone into the tropical region. A cool Coca Cola tasted refreshing. Juan drank the juice from a coconut that was freshly cut and opened for him by a roadside vendor. Once back in the car, Tommy talked with JoAnn about her home, her school, and her experiences with his father's program. Sometimes he spoke in Spanish, and other times in English. Occasionally, Juan offered a comment, but generally he seemed lost in his own thoughts as he steered the car toward their destination. Tommy guessed Juan was at least in his fifties, and that he was bored. The trip for Juan was just another day's work, and certainly it was not the adventure Tommy found it to be.

It was early afternoon when the trio arrived in Canoguitas. The town looked different than Tommy remembered. It appeared larger, dustier, and more impoverished than he recalled. He didn't recognize anything except the road, which led through town towards the unnamed road and his old home. When they came to the unnamed road, Tommy saw the jungle had been pushed back considerably. The car stopped at the compound gate and JoAnn swiftly jumped out and opened the gate wide enough for the car to drive through.

Then she closed the gate and returned to the car. Juan drove a short distance and stopped in front of a building that had a sign *Administration* posted on it. The three climbed out of the car and Tommy noticed the air smelled clean, laden with perfume from the tropical flowers that grew rampant along the compound fence and in well-maintained beds. "Your father's probably in there," JoAnn said, pointing toward the entrance. Then she extended her hand. "Nice meeting you Tommy. We'll have to get together sometime." Tommy nodded and watched as JoAnn turned and walked away. He was delighted to discover he was actually thinking in Spanish again. What he thought was how well JoAnn filled out her tight jeans and how much he would like to get into them.

When Tommy entered the administration building, he was taken aback for a moment. He remembered the night he had found his mother, a broken woman, sobbing on the floor. The room was much as he remembered it, with the same file cabinets, desk, and worktables. The walls were still white, but new posters and artwork hung on them. Behind the large black desk, a woman was working on papers. She looked up when Tommy entered, and smiled. Then she greeted him in English.

"Well," she said, "You must be Tommy. It is so nice to see you again."

Tommy didn't remember ever seeing her before, but he smiled and nodded.

The woman continued. "You probably don't remember me; you were quite young when you left. And I was younger then, too."

Tommy looked closer. She was a small woman, petite and striking, with a lovely face. Her black hair was pulled back in the manner of a Tango dancer. Tommy thought she must be Lila. She had to be; she looked as he imagined she would, but more attractive.

"Are you Lila?" He inquired.

"Of course. We're so happy you have come for a visit. Tonight we are having a fiesta in your honor. The pastor is quite anxious to see you."

"That's nice," replied Tommy. "Can you tell me where my father is?"

"I am afraid he is not here now. He had to go to Quetzaltenango today. That's why we sent JoAnn to pick you up at the airport. But your father will be here this evening. Let me take you to our home. We have a room prepared for you and I'm sure you must be tired."

The house where Lester and his new family lived was new and luxurious compared to the cement block structure of his childhood. The new house matched the church. Both were built in the Spanish style—white stucco and black iron trim with red tiled roofs. The house wrapped around a courtyard in which there was ample room for walking in a small garden. In the center of the courtyard was a fountain. Tommy noticed several maids scurrying back and forth across the courtyard. One maid swept the courtyard floor, while another attempted to shoo a white peacock from the premises. *How is all this possible?* Tommy wondered. *How can Lester afford this fancy new house? Apparently, the ministry has prospered.* Tommy pondered all this as he rested in bed in the room Lila had prepared. Eventually he fell asleep and didn't wake until he heard a tapping on his door. Looking at the clock, he saw it was after five o'clock in the afternoon.

The most unusual thing about the "fiesta dinner" was how unremarkable it was. Tommy was nervous because he didn't know how his father would receive him. Was Lester really as happy about the visit as Lila implied? Now that he was here, Tommy felt uncertain and confused. He had come in anger and defiance, but he now found it difficult to conjure up these emotions. Tommy had believed he didn't care about Lester, but he felt stirrings of old memories of when he and his father had been close. A maid led Tommy back through the house and into the living room where his father stood to greet him. Tommy felt a surge of emotion stronger than any he could recall in many years.

But his feelings were swiftly quelled by Lester's limp handshake and distant manner. There was no warm hug or tears or joy or remorse. A door in Tommy's heart that had tentatively been kept open for just this occasion now quietly closed.

Lila entered the room and greeted Tommy warmly with a kiss to the cheek, "You must meet the children," she said, and then called over a boy and a girl named Miguel and Maggie. The two children approached and respectfully offered their hands to be introduced formally.

"Miguel is seven years old and Maggie is six," Lila continued, "we are very proud of them."

"It's very nice to meet you," Tommy said while shaking their hands.

Lester made a cursory inquiry regarding the welfare of Penny and Tammy, but then quickly turned the conversation to the activities of his ministry. Lila vainly attempted to steer the conversation to more personal topics by asking Tommy about his interests and his future plans, but Lester refused to digress. He appeared more interested in the minutia of the ministry than conversing with a son whom he hadn't seen in eight years. Tommy observed this and feigned indifference. At least he knew where he stood.

Physically, Lester looked much as Tommy remembered—just older and heavier. The hair was thinning and turning silver at the temples. As Tommy listened to Lester he recognized many of his father's expressions and gestures he had forgotten over the years. Not once did Tommy detect warmth or interest from Lester. As he searched the memories of his early childhood, Tommy realized Lester never had been a demonstrative father. The mission always came first with Lester, and any approval or attention Tommy received had hinged on Tommy's ability to be of use—by delivering pamphlets, translating Spanish, or reciting Bible verses. It all seemed so obvious now. It also seemed a bit ironic to Tommy that instead of making him sad or angry, this revelation brought a sense of relief and accomplishment. It was the feeling one gets when he cracks a code or solves a mystery that has been confounding him.

Such were Tommy's thoughts as he calmly listened while Lester explained that the Evangelical Friendship Mission of Guatemala was much more than merely a church and Sunday school. It had grown into a whole support network. Lester could feed the hungry, house the homeless, and then, after the basics were met, minister to the spiritual needs of his people. Lester spoke with authority, as if preaching a sermon. Tommy recalled the four-room hut that had been his father's home eight years earlier, and he concluded Lester was feeding and housing himself right along with the poor he now referred to as "his people." With the detached curiosity of a jaguar appraising its prey, Tommy wondered if Lester had any idea how hypocritical he was. A maid indicated that dinner was ready and they all entered the dinning room. Lester took his seat at the head of the table and began to say grace.

"Thank you, Lord, for thy bounty that is set before us today. Thank you for all our blessings and for bringing young Tommy here to visit with us. Thank you for giving us good health and a successful program. And Lord, I still have the refrigerator. It's an older model but it works well. I have been trying to find a buyer for two weeks and haven't had any serious inquiries. I'd appreciate it if you cold send someone my way. As always, we acknowledge Thee in all things, Lord. In Jesus' name we pray. Amen."

As they ate, Lester continued to describe the demands of running the mission and Tommy felt a stirring of resentment. The delicious food was cooked and served by maids. Every need was attended to, as if those seated at the table were royalty. Tommy realized that Lester and his new family had been living in luxury while his mother had been forced to rely on the charity of her parents in Ohio. Tommy thought of his mother and Grandma Mildred sewing away in the dining room to earn enough money to pay the food bill, while Lila and Lester had lived in their estate with peafowl roaming around the premises. Even Pat O'Brien seemed a sympathetic figure by comparison. Tommy thought of Pat with his red face sweating as he rushed about trying to satisfy a customer or rearrange a display. Tommy was glad that his mom had Pat, so when Lester asked how the family was doing, Tommy could honestly answer, "Great. Thank you. Couldn't be better."

The candlelight on the table highlighted the lines and creases in Lester's face and the age spots beginning to emerge. When the main course was over, one maid cleared the table, and another served coffee and flan. Lester talked more slowly now, and seemed tired. He was still a commanding presence, but less intense. Lila referred to Lester as "her oso" which Tommy knew meant "bear," and it seemed an appropriate name. After gobbling the flan, the bear leaned back and rubbed his belly in satisfaction. That was the happiest Tommy had seen Lester all night.

If Lester was a bear, then Tommy considered Lila a hummingbird—vibrant and exotic, with hands that flittered about as she talked. She was petite though somewhat top heavy with wide eyes and a broad, friendly smile. Her voice was low and musical. Tommy had to keep reminding himself not to stare at her breasts. Lila and Lester sat at opposite ends of the table. Across from Tommy were the two children. Tommy hadn't known Lester had other children, and he wondered if Penny knew. He realized nostalgically that Miguel was not much younger than Tommy had been when he left Guatemala.

Miguel and Maggie were quiet and well mannered through dinner. They were mildly curious about Tommy, but he sensed that no one had explained that he was their half-brother. To them, he was just another guest for dinner, a gringo visiting the mission. The oso didn't show any interest in the children as he rubbed his tummy and droned on about the plight of his people. Tommy smiled at the two tablemates across from him. When given the opportunity, he asked Miguel and Maggie polite but meaningless questions, and tried to appear interested in their answers. At the end of the meal, Miguel and Maggie looked relieved to be excused, and they quickly ran off to play. For a moment Tommy thought about bringing up the subject of Molina, his chicken, but he knew that wouldn't be wise. Besides, he hadn't decided yet what he wanted from Lester.

After coffee, Lester invited Tommy on a tour of the compound. The staff was working again. Lester explained it was customary after a light dinner for staff to return to work until seven or eight o'clock in the evening. It was starting to get dark but in the moonlight it was still easy to see everything. In addition to Lester and Lila's house there were several new buildings that Lester was obviously proud of. He showed Tommy the new church, food bank, and a large structure that served as an emergency shelter and temporary house for people in need. A little further in the background were several small houses, huts really, that were residences for the staff and their families. Tommy noted most of Lester's workers were young Guatemalan women, most of whom were very pretty.

As they entered the administration building, Tommy smiled at two young women, barely more than girls, who were involved with paperwork. Lester explained they were writing letters to sponsors. The sponsors were mainly from the United States, and sent a financial stipend each month to provide for their "foster" child's support. Since most of the children sponsored were too young to read or write, the mission had letter-writers (students studying English at the mission) to write letters by hand on behalf of the children. Their unrefined penmanship and imperfect language gave the letters an authentic quality.

"How many sponsors are there?" Tommy

asked.

"Enough," Lester replied, the scowl indicating that he didn't want to discuss the sponsorship program further.

Lester reminded Tommy of a rooster as he strutted from one building to another, always greeted with reverence by whomever he encountered along the way. *El Patron,* Tommy thought, *the big cheese, a man over-inflated with his own sense of importance.* Tommy smiled as he thought of the mission as nothing more than an elaborate chicken yard, where Lester the rooster stashed his hens. *And I,* Tommy thought, *am the fox that Lester has unwittingly let in.*

Later that night as Tommy lay in bed before falling asleep, he felt his excitement grow. Although he didn't understand Lester—or feel affection for him—Tommy was glad he had come to this place. He felt comfortable here. The climate, the colors, and the memories were genuine. They were not lies. This place felt like home. And during the course of the evening, Tommy had come to realize he and Lester might be very much alike. He saw that Lester was not a man interested in family or God; Lester was interested in maintaining his own little fiefdom in the middle of paradise. And this, Tommy realized, was what he wanted, too. This was what he had missed the past eight years in

Ohio. Lester had once shared the kingdom with Tommy, and then took it all away. Now Tommy wanted it back. But how?

****

Tommy waited and observed, unsure of what he was waiting for. Lester remained distant but unconcerned about Tommy's presence at the mission. Each day Tommy got up early in the morning only to learn that Lester was already gone, often for the day, on "important business." *That sounds familiar,* Tommy thought, remembering when he and Tammy and his mother left Guatemala and Lester was so involved with "business" that he didn't even come home to say goodbye. It seemed little had changed, except that it was now Lila and their two children who took a back seat to Lester's ambition. Tommy believed that the key to gaining Lester's help would not be guilt or the familial bond. What truly mattered to Lester was the mission and his hen yard. After two weeks of observing, a plan began to form—Tommy would make himself indispensable. He would become an asset to the mission. He would begin by making himself useful to Lila.

Since Lester was away from the mission most of the time, Tommy was free to wander around the compound, watching, asking questions and practicing his Spanish. He discovered that Guatemalan women found him even more attractive than the girls in high school. Of course being Lester's son afforded him a social status, even if he wasn't the favorite son. It also didn't hurt that he was North American, athletic, and had amazing blue eyes. But most importantly, Tommy knew how to listen. Just as in Ohio, he would ask a question and then sit back and say little. His silence and concern, along with his striking eyes, invited a wealth of trust and information.

Tommy liked Lila, and went out of his way to please her. He understood why Lester had been so smitten that he was willing to sacrifice Penny and the children. Lila had been a school girl when she first met and attracted Lester. He was teaching the class. Tommy could imagine the sparks flying. Today it was apparent that Lila had an abundance of confidence. She was sensual, nurturing, and playful—a delicious combination of qualities. She doted on her children, and Tommy sometimes found himself jealous of the attention Lila gave to her kids. Tommy won Miguel's devotion by practicing soccer with him. Since Tommy had been a star soccer player in Ohio he was able to teach Miguel some moves. After practicing with Miguel for an hour in the afternoon, he would take the boy and

Maggie, and sometimes Lila, for an ice cream. He drove Lila to the market and helped her around the house and garden. Whatever favor Lila requested, Tommy would graciously do. "It is my pleasure," he would say with exaggerated formality, "to help such a beautiful lady." Lila thanked him by laughing and speaking in her musical voice, and sometimes pressing herself against him in a tight embrace of appreciation. He was glad Lester wasn't around to see such displays. By the end of three weeks in Guatemala, Tommy had come to the conclusion Lila was restless but devoted to Lester when he was around. Lila loved her life in the compound and the role she played as Lester's wife. When her husband was absent, she enjoyed flirting with men, and was well aware of her charms and how to use them. With women, Tommy noticed she was less than kind. In fact, she could be harsh and demanding. She seemed ever watchful when Lester was present, and anxious to meet his every need. Tommy guessed Lila's big fear was one day a younger woman might attempt to supplant her, as she had done to Tommy's mother.

Although Tommy enjoyed Lila's company and attention, he didn't learn much from her—at least not what he most wanted to learn. However, two other women proved useful in this regard: JoAnn (the American intern) and Rosario (a dark-haired local beauty). Rosario worked as a letter writer for the sponsorship program, and JoAnn was the general "gofer" who occasionally gave English lessons. With both women, Tommy was charming and enthusiastically offered his help. He was richly rewarded. By the end of one month, Tommy realized he had learned more about his father's enterprise than Lester would ever have knowingly revealed.

From Rosario, he learned that a lot of money came to the mission through donations and the sponsorship program. There were so many sponsors that the letter writers had difficulty keeping up with the volume of letters and reports that needed to be written. To save time, they wrote the same letter for three or four different children, changing only the names and ages. Most of Lester's day trips were to find and photograph families who qualified for help. Sponsorship had become a major source of income for the mission.

From JoAnn, Tommy learned that Lester was besieged by stress, being pulled in several directions at once. Churches and groups in the United States who provided donations to Lester's mission were demanding. They wanted visits and presentations to show what their money was accomplishing. Lester himself had not traveled to the United States in over a year and a half, so now (at Lester's suggestion) some of his contributors decided to send their own representatives to Guatemala to see for themselves the mission's activities. When in the United States, Lester frequently invited the churchgoers to visit, JoAnn explained, but he never expected they would actually come. As a rule, Lester did not like visits from the outside; he regarded them as an intrusion and an interruption of his real work. However, he realized that catering to the wishes of sponsors was vital to the success of the mission. JoAnn was enlisted to occupy the visitors whenever any showed up and keep them entertained. JoAnn said she loved this aspect of her internship.

Usually the visitors wanted nothing more than to be tourists and see as much of Guatemala as possible. JoAnn would take them to Guatemala City to see the Central Market, the municipal museum, and the zoo. On Thursdays she would drive them to Chichicastenango so they could see the Indian population at the native market. She confided to Tommy that she enjoyed these outings into the country, but with apprehension. She wasn't very familiar with the roads or comfortable with aggressive motorists. The driving in Guatemala, particularly around the city, was crazy. In the countryside there was the matter of unrest among the indigenous people. This occurred mostly in the mountains and in the provinces that JoAnn avoided whenever she could. The government referred to the rebels as guerillas or subversives or communists. Finally, there were the *banditos*, ordinary criminals who sometimes stopped cars and demanded payment from the passengers. Bandits regarded tourists as opportunities.

During the weeks Tommy was at the compound, no one mentioned his leaving Guatemala, and Tommy didn't bring the subject up. He tried to show what contributions he could make so Lester, Lila and the rest of the staff would want him to remain. Whenever Lester was around, Tommy was especially cautious because he knew he had not yet gained Lester's full acceptance or trust. But just as he hoped, Lila and JoAnn began to praise Tommy's helpfulness when they spoke with Lester.

One afternoon, seven weeks after Tommy had arrived, JoAnn invited him and Rosario to accompany her on an outing. She was taking some visitors to Guatemala City and she said she'd feel safer with their company. Both Tommy and Rosario were delighted to be invited.

The visitors were Edward and Beverly Peterson from Chattanooga. Mr. Peterson had worked for the 3M Company for thirty years, and was recently retired. This trip was Mr. Peterson's reward for thirty years of hard work, and it was their first experience traveling outside of the United States. The Peterson's an affable couple, childlike in their enthusiasm. They were wide-eyed and filled with questions as JoAnn drove the minibus through the countryside.

"Some people wear colorful clothing while others don't. Why is that?" asked Mrs. Peterson.

Rosario was the first to answer. "The colorful clothing is worn by the Indian people of Guatemala. They are the descendants of the Maya. They are proud of their apparel. It takes a long time to hand weave and embroider. Wearing the clothes makes them feel special and sets them apart."

"I'll bet you didn't know," JoAnn added, "that their outfits have a specific pattern that is unique to each village. By looking at the cloth pattern you can tell which village a person comes from. If you see two women wearing the same color patterns, they are from the same village. Do you know, Mrs. Peterson, that the Indians don't speak Spanish? They speak their own language. Spanish is the official language of Guatemala but there are twenty-three other Indian languages that are spoken here. The main ones are Quiche and Cakchiquel."

"I didn't know that," Mrs. Peterson answered.

"How do you know all this?" Mr. Peterson

asked.

"In college we studied the history and culture of Guatemala. It was part of my preparation for coming here to work with Brother Lester."

Mrs. Peterson asked, "Do you know any Indians personally?"

"My grandparents are Indian," Rosario answered. "On my father's side—my father too—at least he used to be. They came from El Quiche, which is a province in the mountains. They are like the people you see with the colorful dress. Their children are Indian too, except my father. He married a woman who was not Indian. He met her while working on a *finca*, a large farm. She was very poor like the Indians. She spoke Spanish and taught my dad to speak Spanish. She didn't want to be regarded as Indian. Gradually my father changed. Now he's just a regular Guatemalan."

"A Ladino," JoAnn added.

"Ladino?" Mrs. Peterson inquired.

"That is what the rest of the people are called—the ones who don't regard themselves as Indian. Some are descended from the Spanish conquistadors, or from Indians who married them or their descendants. They developed their own unique culture. In the U.S. you might call such people mestizos. They are referred to as Ladinos or Latinos but mostly, just Guatemalans."

"And that is why, Rosario, you don't wear the handmade clothing?" Mrs. Peterson inquired.

"Yes. It takes a long time to make such clothing. Most Guatemalans wear regular clothes like everyone else."

"Could you wear the Indian clothing if you wanted?" Mrs. Peterson continued. "I think you would look precious. You're so young and pretty."

"Thank you, Mrs. Peterson. I could wear the clothing but it would be disrespectful. It is theirs and it makes them feel special. I would not feel comfortable. But thank you for your kind remarks."

"Are the Indians treated the same as other Guatemalans?" Mr. Peterson asked.

"According to what I learned at college," JoAnn replied, "the answer is no. They don't have the opportunities other people in Guatemala have. They are a minority culture within a dominant culture. Their hours are long and their wages low. The conditions of their employment are sometimes harsh. But they have to settle for whatever work they can get. Think of it! Most don't even speak Spanish. There is prejudice here and Indians are looked down upon and treated poorly."

"Unfortunately," Rosario continued, "JoAnn is right. The Indians are a humble people. Recently some have begun to fight so the rest of the world will learn of their situation. They feel that there is no place for them in their own country. They are discriminated against. Their land has been stolen from them for five hundred years. Piece by piece it has been taken away, leaving them with the inhospitable land high in the mountains—land that nobody else wants. But some want it now. A few Indians are so angry they have become violent. What the government calls guerillas, the Indians call resistance fighters."

"I had no idea you were both so politically-minded," said Tommy.

"I got an A in college," said JoAnn, "in my course on Central American Culture."

Then Tommy turned to Rosario and asked, "How did you learn to speak English so well?"

"I learned English in school. But I also read in English. I've always enjoyed reading since I was a little girl. I know about the Indians mostly because of my father. I feel connected to the Indian people, even if he doesn't."

For a while they drove in silence, enjoying the scenery.

"We've been sponsoring a Guatemalan child for five years," Mrs. Peterson said. "I believe we have done some good—at least I hope so."

"I'm sure you have," Rosario answered.

"Why do you think Guatemalans are so short?" asked Mrs. Peterson. The question was so abrupt that nobody knew how to answer. Finally Tommy said, "Why do you have brown hair? You just do. You were born that way."

Again there was silence for a long time. Finally the car entered the outskirts of Guatemala City, and they headed toward the city market. Mr. and Mrs. Peterson were looking for souvenirs to take back to Chattanooga. The Central Market was a large maze of vendors, each with their wares crammed into small stalls. There were hundreds of cubicles within a large permanent structure under one roof. The market was the size of a football field, with two levels. Other more makeshift and scattered stalls spilled outside the market on the street. The place was noisy and congested with people. "Watch your wallets and don't wear jewelry," JoAnn advised. "There are pickpockets here. Let's plan to meet back at this spot in about an hour, okay?" Everyone agreed and they took off in different directions. Joann and the Petersons headed toward the center of the marketplace. They would all stay together so JoAnn could translate for them. Rosario followed Tommy as he ambled outside around the perimeter.

It was a warm day, and after fifteen minutes or so of walking about, Tommy bought Rosario a Coke from a street vendor. It was served Guatemalan style, in a plastic bag with a straw sticking out.

When she finished her beverage they entered the market starting their journey on the ground floor. They continued to walk until Tommy stopped at a booth selling leather goods. He was examining a sandal when Rosario stepped up beside him and spoke softly, barely audible.

"You might be a father."

Tommy didn't think he heard her correctly. He put down the sandal he was holding. "What did you say?"

"I said you might be a father. It's still early, but I think it's possible."

Tommy didn't respond. He stared at the table of shoes, as if they held an answer.

"I might be pregnant," she whispered, more urgently.

"Oh." Tommy felt his stomach knot. "How do you know?"

"My regla... I missed it." Rosario glanced around nervously, but no one near them was paying attention to the English conversation at the sandal stand.

"You missed your period?" Tommy asked, stalling for time. He wished he could run away, but he feared his feet wouldn't move.

Rosario nodded. She looked at him intently.

Tommy didn't know what to say. "And you're sure it's mine?"

"Yes, Tommy, it is yours." Rosario's glare didn't falter, and Tommy sensed a hardness forming as her dark eyes bored into his. He took a deep breath.

"How do you know?" he asked, looking away from the heat that now burst forth. He could feel sparks flying from her eyes and knew she was still staring at him, forming her response. He picked up another sandal and studied it carefully.

"I know because there is no one else." Her voice sounded surprisingly calm.

"So," Tommy asked, "what do you want me to do? Do you want money? Do you want me to marry you?"

"I want or expect nothing. I thought you should know. That's all."

Tommy tossed the sandal down, annoyed. "Well, I guess I know."

Rosario never had the opportunity to reply further because at that moment the Petersons and JoAnn emerged from a side isle. They lumbered forward in single file, each laden with bags of goods.

"Hey amigos, look what we got." Mr. Peterson said, lifting up the mounted head of a bull. "This is going on the wall above our fireplace."

"Wow. That's something," Tommy said, grateful for the interruption. "It's sort of big. It may be difficult to carry on an airplane." Then he turned toward JoAnn, and whispered in Spanish, "Have you ever seen anything so ugly?"

"What was that?" Mr. Peterson asked.

"Nothing," Tommy said. "I was just remarking that it's an interesting souvenir."

"Yes, it is that," Mr. Peterson said smiling.

With their shopping complete, the five of them headed back to the minibus. They were all hungry, and JoAnn suggested that the Hotel Pan American would be a good spot to eat before returning to the compound. It offered superb cuisine with plenty of ambiance. All the waiters and waitresses wore the indigenous costumes of the Maya, and JoAnn knew it would be the perfect ending for the Petersons' adventure. They ate a traditional Guatemalan meal with black beans and rice and fried plantains. Throughout the meal, a small band played traditional music, and the quiet spells were filled in by more questions from the Petersons.

On the return trip home, Rosario remained quiet, but no one seemed to notice. Both Tommy and JoAnn continued the nonstop chatter with the Petersons who were thrilled with the outing. Mr. Peterson kept stroking his bull head, and Tommy decided the old man couldn't be prouder if he had bagged a lion on safari.

****

For the next week Tommy avoided Rosario, and hoped she would just disappear. Once he came upon her by accident, and she quickly lowered her head and walked away. Nothing more was said about the pregnancy. One part of Tommy felt badly, but he didn't know what to do or say. He couldn't afford this type of problem right now; it wasn't part of his plan. In the end, Tommy blamed Rosario for the situation. She should have known better and taken precautions. *Was she trying to trap me?* Even though he had no evidence, he was quite sure he wasn't the first man she had ever been with, so why should he get stuck with the bill? Women had ways to take care of these things. Maybe she had already taken care of it. Rosario had said she wanted nothing, and that was fine with him. She would get her wish.

The following week Tommy was playing soccer with Miguel when JoAnn suddenly appeared on the lawn. "I need to talk to you," she said, "when you have some time." Tommy felt his stomach sink. His first thought was that JoAnn knew about Rosario's pregnancy. *The bitch probably said something. This could jeopardize everything. I'll just deny. That will be my defense, the Tuttle defense— lie and deny. It will be her word against mine.* Then a worse thought came to mind: *Could JoAnn be pregnant, too? That would do it!*

Tommy excused himself from Miguel, and nervously walked with JoAnn across the yard expecting the worst to happen.

"I have an idea," JoAnn said, "Why don't you apply to Theophilus College? I really think you'd like it. You could study to do the kind of work your dad does. You could work part-time for the mission and get a degree at the same time. And we could continue to see each other."

Tommy was overwhelmed with relief, and upon reflection he liked JoAnn's idea. But what about the finances? He thought he could count on Pat for some of his expenses. He could even work part time if he had to. But would Lester go for it? Would his father help? Would Lester even want to remain connected to him? Tommy wasn't sure. Lately Lester seemed friendly, but Tommy really didn't know how Lester felt about him. Tommy reasoned that asking Lester for help was worth a try. If Lester cared for him at all, he would offer help; if Lester wanted to get rid of him, he still might offer money just to get Tommy out of Guatemala.

When Tommy summoned up the courage to speak to Lester about Theophilus, he was happily surprised. Lester was in a particularly good mood because he had finally sold the refrigerator. Lester listened intently as Tommy explained the idea, and then he agreed.

"College is important. It opens doors. I wish I had been given the opportunity to go to college. I had to get my education through correspondence courses. That's not the same as really attending classes. And Theophilus College is an excellent choice. You will get a good Christian foundation there. Who, knows? When you're finished maybe you can join our team and work here. But that's not important. You'll be grounded in the faith and there will be plenty of opportunities for you. I think you have a good idea and I would like to help. I didn't help much when you were growing up in Ohio, but maybe I can make up for that now." This was the first indication that Lester felt any closeness toward Tommy. "I can write a letter of reference. Brother McPherson, the president of Theophilus, is a friend of mine. I'll recommend you for a scholarship."

It was more than Tommy had hoped for. His goal now seemed within reach. One day he would have his own kingdom, or this kingdom might be his. The last two weeks of Tommy's stay in Guatemala flew by quickly because he was so excited about his future. With each passing day he felt a greater resolve. *I was right*, he thought, *I belong in Guatemala. This is where I started from and this is where I am meant to be.* His adventure in Guatemala had lasted a total of nine weeks. He believed them to be the most important nine weeks of his life.

Tommy said his goodbyes and left Canoguitas for Guatemala City to catch a flight back to the United States. As he waited in the departure lounge, he noticed some fliers scattered throughout the waiting area. They turned out to be newsletters from an introduction service named *Friends of All Nations.* It listed women wanting to meet men from North America for "friendship and possible marriage." There were pages with pictures of young women from Panama, Honduras, Guatemala, and other Latin American countries. Tommy studied the pictures. There were several girls he found attractive and whom he would like to meet. But in order to meet them, he had to first pay a fee to the service. Then, supposedly, the organization would facilitate correspondence with the women Tommy chose. Tommy folded the newsletter. *Why not?* He thought. *What harm can it do?* He stuffed the newsletter into his carry-on bag just as the announcement was being made to board the airplane for Houston.

10
LIFE IN A BUBBLE

Tommy was a good student at Theophilus. He studied hard, and enjoyed learning. He was also one of their best athletes, a varsity player for the *Fighting Friends*. Although he wasn't tall, Tommy was wiry and fast and his speed made up for what he lacked in height. Tommy was popular and liked by other students and his instructors. He had one mishap during second semester when he and a buddy decided to see a movie in town and they were seen leaving the theater. This was a serious rule infraction. Movies were "of the world" and consequently not permitted. Tommy and his friend had to make a public apology to the student body. It was a humiliating event for Tommy, made worse by the fact that it occurred shortly before a speaking engagement by his father. When Lester arrived on campus and learned of the incident, he was livid.

"How could you be so thoughtless? You can't afford such mistakes in judgment. Remember, you don't just represent yourself; your actions reflect on the entire mission—and on me. What about your testimony?"

"You're right," Tommy responded. "I'm sorry. It was a stupid mistake. I apologized to the student body and now I'm apologizing to you. "

A man who prays to sell a refrigerator, thought Tommy.

But Lester was not satisfied. "Stop making excuses. There's no place for such an attitude at the mission. It's not up to you to decide which rules to obey or not. If you don't understand this, then you are of no use to me or the mission."

"I really am sorry, Dad. In the future I'll think before I act." Inwardly, Tommy was angry with himself. He must be more careful. Following the rules at Theophilus was harder than he had imagined. Sometimes he felt he would explode if he didn't get away. Tommy decided the next time he wanted to see a movie he would go to another city where nobody from Theophilus would see him. *I've learned a lesson,* he thought. *Don't get caught. Be more careful. I won't make that mistake again.*

****

Theophilus wasn't like most colleges, and its students were different, too. In the real world beyond Theophilus, students were advocating for civil rights, burning flags, and protesting the Vietnam War. Theophilus was a cocoon and within it the Friends of God (the students) were on their own spiritual quests that were inner-directed.

They were not concerned with the problems of the world. So when race riots broke out in Newark and Detroit and later spread to Washington D.C., there was little notice or concern at Theophilus. The students of Theophilus had no awareness of the Summer of Love or of the publication of the first list of animals to be officially declared endangered. They were not interested in politics, animals or the environment. They were interested in spiritual matters and current events only when they impacted the interpretation of scripture. For this reason, they were acutely aware of Israel's Six Day War. Israel mattered because the nation of Israel had a special place in God's plan. The covenants between God and Israel were everlasting. The Jews, being the covenant people of God, held special significance. One day God would restore the Kingdom to Israel. At that time, the Christians and the Jews would share in salvation and the House of Jacob would be ruled over by the Son of the Most High, as stated in the Gospel of Luke. Therefore, faculty and students discussed what was happening in the Middle East and studied it at great length. It was, after all, the fulfillment of prophecy. All of God's prophecies needed to be fulfilled before Jesus Christ would return to Earth and establish His kingdom. That is what prophecy and the subject of eschatology was about: the last days, the end of time. Tommy found eschatology fascinating although it was one of the more difficult subjects he studied at Theophilus.

Tommy didn't let the turbulent times of the 1960s bother him. He kept his attention on the things that mattered. He went to class, he read his Bible, and attended services. For fun he played sports and dated. During his first semester, he reunited with JoAnn, and, except for a few indiscretions, they dated exclusively for a year. But she was a senior so the romance was brief. When JoAnn left Nashville for a teaching job, Tommy started dating other women. Just like in high school he did most of the listening, and let the women talk. The college girls weren't different from those in high school. They talked about similar things, except now they just talked more. But at the last minute instead of asking if he loved them, the girls at Theophilus would pose a question like "What would God want us do?" or "What would God think?" *He would think you're a complete moron,* Tommy thought.

Sometimes Tommy wondered if getting laid was worth all the effort. Even when he succeeded, he constantly worried about what would happen if one of the girls suddenly repented her sins and named Tommy as the man who influenced her disgraceful behavior. Even worse, what if one got pregnant? That would do it as far as Lester was concerned. Tommy sometimes wondered about

Rosario. How did she explain her pregnancy? Did she get rid of the baby? Tommy had no idea, and no way to find out. He knew he would never be allowed to return to the mission if Lester learned the truth. Eventually Tommy settled for a couple of women from town who worked late into the night at the Go-Go Club. They were free during the day, so Tommy could sneak out for a couple of hours in the afternoon and still be back at school before curfew.

After JoAnn left, there was one student at Theophilus who fascinated Tommy. Her name was Grace Spindler. She was a freshman with blond hair and bright blue eyes. She had smooth, creamy skin, rosy cheeks, and she always seemed to be smiling— as if in possession of some private secret. She wore her hair in a ponytail that swung from side to side as she dashed across campus or hurried to one of her extracurricular activities. Grace seemed to be involved in just about everything at Theophilus. Even though she was only a freshman, she stood out from other girls because of her beauty, her energy, and her unswerving sense of purpose. Grace believed she was destined to serve the Lord as a missionary. Theophilus College was the means to fulfilling that destiny.

Grace never looked for ways to get around the rules. She didn't mind wearing the hem of her skirt at her ankles or taking a chaperone with her if she dated. Grace accepted that rules were important; the school wouldn't have rules if they weren't necessary. Grace was serious about religion; it wasn't just lip service with her. She was a Christian whose path lay before her as clear as the Yellow Brick Road.

To Tommy, Grace was a worthy challenge. She was pretty, but seemed oblivious to her appeal. Or maybe she just didn't care. She was not interested in romance, and Tommy was certain she knew little about men because she never responded like other girls did. She was more playful than flirty. When he tried one night to smooth her hair in hopes he might make out with her, she pushed his hand away. Then she looked him directly in the eye and launched into a discussion of eschatology.

"Tommy, do you think we are in the 70th week of Daniel's prophecy?"

"What?"

"If Israel takes control of Jerusalem and signs a peace agreement with Egypt or Syria, then I believe we will be in the 70th week of Daniel's prophecy. That means Jesus could come at any time!"

"I suppose," replied Tommy. He had finally managed to get Grace to sit in his car with him. There was no chaperone present, which was in itself a violation of Theophilus' rules. It took a lot of convincing to get Grace to go so far and Tommy didn't want to waste this opportunity. He tried to draw her closer to him, but she was rigid.

"We must watch and wait. Jesus will come and we must be ready. We must keep ourselves worthy. I hope you have been soul-winning."

Tommy leaned back in exasperation. This seduction attempt was bound to fail. He had never known anyone so preoccupied with thoughts of a spiritual life. Even though he was frustrated by Grace's attitude, Tommy was not discouraged. She presented a challenge, which made her even more appealing. He was convinced Grace was great wife material. *This is the kind of woman I need— someone Dad will approve of who can share my work in Guatemala.*

"I'm so excited," Grace continued. "Imagine! We are living our lives in the end of times. It's positively historic. You do believe in premillennialism—don't you?"

"Of course Grace. But to be honest, I don't think a millennial position is all that important."

"Not important! How can you say that? It's our doctrine."

"Yeah, but it really doesn't change anything, does it? What will be, will be. It's going to happen no matter what your millennial position. It reminds me of the story about the blind men and the elephant."

"What are you talking about?"

"It's like this." Tommy dug deep in the recesses of his memory to recall something he heard in one of his classes. "Three blind men are asked to touch an elephant and describe it. Each man touches a different part. One touches the tail and says an elephant is like a rope. Another touches it in the middle and describes it as a wrinkled old man. The third touches a tusk and says it is hard like a stone.

"Each is correct, but each is describing the elephant from a different perspective; from what they perceive. Now, say you are talking about doctrine. One person reads the Bible and comes to one conclusion. He believes Jesus will come and rule for one thousand years—that's you, a premillennialist. Another person interprets the Bible differently. He takes the position that the one thousand years doesn't mean literally a thousand years. It should be interpreted figuratively. It is a long period of time, but not necessarily one thousand actual years. After this long period of time passes, however long it is, the Lord will return—that's a postmillennialist. Then there is the person who believes there is no one-thousand-year kingdom on Earth at all. He's called an amillennialist. Who's right? Who knows? Maybe they are all right. Each is interpreting scripture differently based on what they read and what they understand. They are like the three blind men with the elephant; each sees things a little differently, but all are honestly trying to describe the same thing."

"That's just crazy," Grace replied. "They can't all be right. There is a right way and a wrong way—in everything. Besides, Scripture is not an elephant."

"Well," said Tommy, "you must admit there's a lot in the Bible that can be confusing. If you cherry-pick what you read you can support practically any doctrinal position you want. Besides, what difference does it make? What will be, will be."

"No. No," Grace insisted. Her ponytail swung as she shook her head. "The Bible is not confusing. It is the inspired word of God. If we misunderstand something, it's from our own weakness, not anything that is wrong with the Bible. And it does make a difference, Tommy. It's important to be correct on doctrine."

"Yeah, I know. But the Bible has been translated and copied many times, from one language into another. Parts were written in Hebrew, parts in Aramaic, parts in Koine Greek. And then these parts were translated into Latin and finally into English. Any one of the copyists or translators could have made a mistake."

"No. That can't be. The Holy Spirit inspired the copyists. The Holy Spirit doesn't make mistakes."

Tommy could see Grace was becoming upset. Next she would be angry with him. "Alright Grace. You're probably right." He didn't want to frustrate her more than he already had. The fact was she was far more spiritual than he. In class he had difficulty following discussions on millennial positions. Besides, he was forgetting his rule about listening. "You're much more evolved spiritually than I am," Tommy said.

"That's not a word I would use," replied Grace. "Evolved means evolution, and I don't believe in evolution."

"I know. You're right; I apologize. What I mean is that you're on a higher spiritual plane than I am. That's all."

If they were talking about soccer or basketball, it would be different. Instead he was running his mouth and should know better. Grace probably was right, anyway. That's what he admired about her. She was so sure of herself and her piety was genuine. Anyone who was that committed probably was correct. *She will make a great missionary wife*, Tommy thought.

By the time Tommy was a senior, he and Grace had put their doctrinal differences aside. They still disagreed frequently, but it was fun, playful banter. Through all their arguing, they told everybody that they were an example of how "opposites attract."

Tommy reasoned that there was a type of girl to fool around with and another type to marry. Grace was in the latter camp. If the arguments became too tedious and it stopped being fun, Tommy would leave Grace for a while and find something else to do. At such times he usually went to the Go Go Club. Other times he would write to one of his "friends" from Latin America. He had received some addresses of women through the international introduction service he had discovered at the airport in Guatemala. Now he had three women with whom he regularly corresponded. Two were from Guatemala and one was from Honduras. In his letters, he lied about himself and what his life was like in the United States. He sent the letters to a mail forwarding service in Miami and the service forwarded the responses to him.

When Tommy graduated from Theophilus, his father flew from Guatemala to attend the ceremony. Penny and Patrick came, too. They were all proud of Tommy. Tommy further thrilled his family by announcing his engagement to

Grace. Penny wept and Lester winked approvingly at Tommy. Even though the wedding was a year away, Lester expressed delight that Tommy and Grace planned to enter the mission field together, and that they hoped to start their married life by serving with him in Guatemala.

The year Tommy graduated had been a good year for him. It was filled with purpose and the promise of things to come. It was a good year for other people too, but for different reasons. The first troops were being withdrawn from Vietnam, and before the year was finished, 75,000 troops would be sent home. The Woodstock Music and Arts Festival attracted more than 300,000 enthusiasts, although Tommy wasn't even aware of its existence. On July 21, 1969, Tommy knew Neil Armstrong walked on the moon because this was the same date he and Grace finalized their plans for a June wedding to be held in Gadsden, Alabama, at the church Grace attended as a child.

11
SACRIFICE

"To Ensure Peace in the Afterlife: When the soul of a person who has passed away needs to be saved, the curandero practices a ritual of cutting off the head of a black chicken. This sacrifice ensures salvation and that the soul of the departed will have a smooth journey to the afterlife." (from Felicita's recipe book)

Both of my mothers were Catholic... in a loose sort of way. But they each also had a separate spiritual source. For Felicita, it was the spells of the curandero; for Mia, it was her Jewish ancestry. The power of mysticism and sacrifice was in their blood. As a child, Mia went to Mass with her father, but her mother was Jewish, and as Mia explained it, "When I met your father in Israel I realized who I was and where I belonged. I didn't want to assimilate and disappear or lose my identity."

I think she was right. It's important to know who you are. Just like if you're Irish... you can't one day decide you're not going to be Irish anymore. Or like me and Felicita... we can't decide not to be Mayan. You can pretend to be someone who you're not, but inside you always know.

The puzzle Mia faced in life involved religion, but not in the same way as my father's dilemma. For ten years Mia struggled with infertility, often doubting if she would ever be a mother. She went through years of sadness, depression, and anger. She wondered if she was being punished for something. Had she failed some grand moral test that she wasn't aware of? She worried that Daniel might not love her if she couldn't bear a child, and sometimes she felt like a failure as a woman. But through it all, she prayed. No matter how angry or discouraged she got, she never turned her back on God.

Her faith was challenged, but she didn't give up. This was her test and her triumph: she called out to any god within hearing range. And the moment her prayers were answered, she didn't hesitate for a second. She said "Thank you, God," booked a flight from Michigan, and flew to Guatemala to claim me.

I asked her once what it was like the first time she saw me. Did she know I was her daughter? Did she love me right away? Mia told me that the day she met me at the airport in Guatemala City was the most wonderful day of her life. When she first looked into my eyes, she said she felt her soul smile. I know what she means because that's exactly what happened to me when I looked into my daughter's eyes for the first time.

Felicita never looked into my eyes, so our souls didn't get a chance to see one another or smile. We remained strangers. I know she was Catholic because she left me a Saint Christopher medal and she wrote that she was Catholic on the forms she completed for the Evangelical Friendship Mission. But she also left me her book of spells. Grace wasn't sure what to do with the book; she was a very religious person and feared it might be of the devil. But Grace cared for Felicita and wanted to honor her friend's wishes. In the end, friendship won out and I received the legacy of two religions, plus a little Mayan magic. Mia and I often read through the book together and tried to decipher its meaning.

I'll never know the puzzle of Felicita's life, but I can tell from her face in the photograph that she was well on her way to grappling with it when I was born. I can't help but wonder if I was her puzzle—the mountain she had to climb. I'm sure I must have been part of it. But when I traveled with Grace through villages in Guatemala, I realized for the first time that just living can sometimes be a challenge—surviving and staying human is an accomplishment. I entered tiny huts with dirt floors and nothing inside except some chairs, hammocks and cooking utensils. Women looked out through doorways with suspicious eyes and hesitant smiles—so many Felicitas. Dusty children, barely 6 or 7 years old with protruding abdomens and limbs like sticks, offered to shine shoes on street corners or followed strangers begging for money. I saw settlements with no utilities where clothes were washed in a river and water was carried daily up steep slopes. Perhaps I wasn't Felicita's puzzle; perhaps I was her prayer. I hope so, but there is no way to know because I've never been able to find her to ask. I do know without a doubt that Felicita's decision to leave me at the Evangelical Friendship Mission most likely saved my life.

The day after my grandfather's funeral, Mia ordered two dozen baby black chickens from a hatchery in Missouri. They were called Black Orpingtons. She turned the back half of our garden shed into a chicken coop and spent the winter tending to her flock. There was a permanent path between walls of snow that she walked each day to feed the chicks and bring water. At night the little shed glowed with an orange/yellow light from the heat lamp for her birds—it looked like a fire blazed inside the coop. The next summer, Mia designated a day of sacrifice for her father. She picked out a bird for Grandpa's sacrifice, and then asked me if I wanted to sacrifice a chicken for my birth mother,

Felicita, because, as she said, "you never know. It can't hurt."

It was quite a sight—the two of us chasing our chosen birds around the chicken yard. They must have sensed our intentions because the otherwise docile fowls suddenly became frantic, knocking over feeders and bouncing off the wire fence. While Mia and I were ducking and screaming, a couple of determined birds managed to push the door open wide enough for half the flock to escape before we realized what had happened. In the end, we held two birds, but were pretty sure they weren't the right ones. Once caught, the birds settled down in the crook of our arms while we cooed and soothed them. The two captives looked up at us trustingly as we turned around surveying the damage.

"Well," Mia said, "I can't do it. I can't kill this bird."

"Me either," I replied. "They're our friends, and they give us eggs." Then we both burst out laughing and let our bird friends go. By nightfall, the rest of the flock returned to the coop, led by the glowing light within. They didn't seem to hold a grudge and life with chickens resumed as normal. Since then I've never been without black chickens— in one form or another. I have porcelain chickens in every room in my house. They bring me joy and I think Felicita would be pleased.

Jim & Cheryl Pahz

12
THE GIRL FROM THE DOGHOUSE

Tommy felt relief as the plane lifted off the runway. There were a few seconds when he noted a sensation of heaviness, and then he felt the plane catch and smoothly rise upwards through a smudge of clouds. He always felt the same way after a conference—relieved and eager to flee. As "Brother Tommy," he served as an ambassador for his father's mission. He would entertain crowds with slides and stories of Guatemala to raise funds for the mission. This was one duty Lester had willingly relinquished. Lester confessed he was tired of traveling and didn't like speaking to crowds. He especially didn't like leaving Guatemala. He was glad to hand those reins to Tommy.

For three days in Minnesota, Tommy had performed nonstop, putting on a "a really big show" as Ed Sullivan would say. The conference was a success, and he was returning to the mission with a briefcase full of pledges. *It's all about marketing. Lester will be proud.* Tommy was exhausted.

Following their wedding five years earlier, Tommy and Grace moved to Guatemala, and Tommy became "Brother Tommy." At the mission, he gradually insinuated himself into all aspects of its operation, assuming more and more responsibilities. He now supervised the sponsorship program and edited the monthly newsletter. Things were good between him and Lester, and more and more Lester revealed the inner workings of the ministry. They were becoming a true father and son team.

Guatemala was home, and whenever Tommy left the country on behalf of the mission, he couldn't wait to return. Although life was sweet, his one disappointment was Grace; she had not turned out to be the wife and helpmate he had expected. She didn't understand him. All Grace seemed interested in was lying in bed, or spending time with the children. She treated Tommy like he was just another child. He resented her nagging, telling him how he should be and what he should do, as if she had her own personal pipeline to God. Tommy found her piety tedious and thought she was ungrateful and lazy. The simple truth was, Grace was not fun. She was depressing to be around, so he began to leave her alone. That was probably what she wanted anyway. Grace certainly didn't appreciate his hard work or accomplishments.

Tommy leaned back in the airplane seat, and yawned. He'd been a good boy in Minnesota, for three long days. Now he was ready to relax and let his hair down. He deserved a little reward—fringe benefits. As the plane soared toward home,

Tommy felt a tug inside—the familiar desire for adventure pulling him like an ocean current—and he made no effort to escape its grip. Tingling with anticipation, he closed his eyes and tried to imagine his encounter with the girl. Her name was Yadira. She was eighteen, but looked younger in the photograph she had sent. Like most of the women whose ads he responded to, she had large, dark eyes and long black hair. He could hardly wait to see her in person.

At the airport in Guatemala City, Tommy rented a car, placed his luggage in the trunk, and headed southeast toward the coast. As he descended the mountains, he felt the rising humidity. The air became increasingly thick and sticky, but he didn't mind. "Bad-boy time," he said. He smiled as he thought of his upcoming adventure.

From the first time he had responded to an ad in the *Friends of All Nations* newsletter, he had loved reinventing himself for different women. Each time he would assume a new persona. He enjoyed planning his new identities and concocting outrageous stories. The exchange of letters and subsequent meetings were exciting. He was a consummate liar and proud of it. This particular excursion would delay his arrival home, but he didn't care. Why hurry? Grace would be there whenever he got home with her hound-dog face and list of grievances. They were totally mismatched and Tommy realized he should never have married her. But he did, and now there were children to think of. If he were Henry the Eighth, he'd just lop off her head and be done with it. Unfortunately he wasn't the king of England. He was just Tommy, so he tried to make the best of his situation. One thing was certain: he would never abandon his children. He would never be like Lester.

Tommy had already written to Yadira, telling her that some day he would come to Guatemala. The trap had been baited; now it was time to see if it would work. *Time to be naughty.*

****

Santa Barbara was a typical Guatemalan village. Located in a poor, rural area, it consisted of small shops and street stalls with dirt roads radiating outward from the town square. Tommy parked the rental car in the town center and walked to a small cantina. Once inside, he took a seat and gazed outside through a dirty window. On the dusty street a boy rode a skinny, downtrodden horse. Next, a rickety cart loaded with melons pulled by a donkey came into view. The scene reminded him of a frontier town from a western movie.

After ordering an Orange Crush, Tommy reached into his jacket pocket and took out the last letter he had received from Yadira. Her letter was one of several he kept in a secret file hidden from Grace. He called it his "slimy dog file," and he smiled whenever he thought of it. He had written Yadira several times, the last being three months ago. He always made sure to use a mail forwarding service so his letters would be postmarked from the United States. In his original correspondence, he told Yadira he was an independently wealthy North American with a lot of time on his hands. He said he was a widower and, since the passing of his beloved wife, he was depressed and lonely. He took a sip of his drink, and unfolded the letter.

Dear Mr. Tommy,

Thank you for the letter. It always make me feel very good to hear you. Thank you for you told me I am pretty.

Your words embarrass me much, but your letters too make me feel special. Yes, I would love to meet you, but Santa Barbara is very far away from your home in the United States. If someday you decide you come to Guatemala, I will love meet and make your acquaintance for fun and good times together. I understand pain you feel since passing of your dead wife. I feel sorry for heart pain. Until then, I remain your devoted friend in romance and possible future times together.

Love always,
Yadira

Tommy smiled as he reread the words. In the last letter he had written her, he asked if she thought there could be a future for the two of them. Would she mind, he wrote, if he came to Guatemala, to Santa Barbara, to meet her personally? He knew it was far, but what were a few thousand miles between such good friends? Wasn't love worth a gamble? Blah, blah, blah… The whole correspondence was so absurd that Tommy chuckled when he thought of it. But he had discovered that regardless of how ridiculous his letters were, the women always believed him. Each new identity was more farfetched, and it was becoming increasingly difficult to outdo himself. Pretty soon he would have to pose as Superman, or maybe a movie star like Steve McQueen. *I am indeed a slimy dog,* he thought.

As expected, Yadira took the bait. How could

she not? She had placed the ad because she wanted to meet someone and escape this dusty town in the middle of nowhere and her life of third-world poverty. She hoped to live happily ever after in *El Norte—Gringo Land,* where money grew on trees and everybody drove big new cars. If it could happen to Cinderella, it could happen to her. All she needed was a prince. Maybe she had found one at last.

Tommy told himself that he was doing this for Yadira; he was providing a few brief moments of happiness in an otherwise dreary existence. He could not use his last name, of course, not his real last name. Nor could he reveal that he lived just a few hours away, or that he was married with two small children. He would play the fantasy out for this short time. She would have this encounter to cherish and look back on to brighten her days. Afterwards it would take her awhile to realize it was make-believe. It would be over before she ever knew what had happened. He liked to move in quickly and exit just as fast. *Just like Speedy Gonzales*, he thought, *whoever that was.* The thought amused him because there was a Manuel Gonzales in his community and he was the slowest dumb-ass that anyone could imagine. Then he thought again of Yadira. She would always have the memories of these few days of happiness. It was his gift to her.

It didn't take Tommy long to locate Yadira's house. After learning that she was working in the fields harvesting sugar cane, Tommy went to the one hotel in town. It was a faded turquoise structure, and sat on a beach with black sand. Tommy was relived to see the hotel had a restaurant. That made things easier. The restaurant was empty now except for some cheerful radio music playing in the background. It looked better than he had expected, but smelled of smoke and stale beer. After he checked out the restaurant he went to the front desk and paid for a room. Then he returned to Yadira's house. He left a note with a maid explaining that he had come to Santa Barbara to meet Yadira. The note said:

My Dear Yadira,

I am here. Can you have dinner with me tonight? I am staying at the Del Centro Hotel. I will be waiting for you in the dining room at seven p.m. I look forward to seeing you. I know this is short notice. Please try to come.

Your friend,
Tommy

He smiled as he left Yadira's house, imagining her astonishment when she learned the wealthy gringo had actually come to this place. She had probably assumed there was as much a chance of that happening as there was of winning the national lottery.

At seven o'clock, there were two other patrons in the restaurant. The dining room had white stucco walls and a terra cotta tile floor. The tables and chairs were mismatched pieces, all in dark wood. Decorating the walls were hand-carved, wooden masks, painted bright colors. The masks were of people and animals; they were a common tourist item at the native markets throughout Guatemala. Tommy sat beneath the mask of a jaguar. During the day the dining room had appeared stark, but now there was a warm glow from the candlelight. From the clothing of the two other people in the room, Tommy guessed they were locals. There were no tourists at the hotel, and Tommy doubted there ever were. Most likely the hotel was originally built for employees and families of the Dole Fruit Company.

He was thinking this when he looked up and saw her. She appeared in the doorway—a vision in a red, floor-length satin gown, as if she was dressed for the senior prom. As in her photograph, she looked younger than eighteen. She had long black hair that hung straight over her shoulders. On her left shoulder strap she wore a white corsage. She was far prettier than her picture suggested, and for a moment she took his breath away. He walked to the entrance to meet her, and then escorted her to her seat. As they walked together toward the table he imagined how ridiculous and out of place they must appear in this forsaken little restaurant. Tommy gave no indication of his amusement at this image. Instead he played his part, making polite conversation, as if they were in a five-star restaurant. "I learned Spanish," he said, "in school. Can you speak any English? How did you get your letters translated into English?" He told her to order whatever she wanted from the sparse menu. "Pay no attention to the price. This is a very special day for me."

As usual, his plan went as expected. After dinner they went to his hotel room and he persuaded her to spend the night. They slept together and the sex was good. It wasn't great, but it was pretty good. He wondered if it could have been her first time, but he didn't think so, nor did he care.

The next morning Tommy felt romantic and he held her hand as he walked her home after breakfast. Now it was his turn to be surprised. Yadira didn't actually live in the house where he had left the note with a maid. She lived behind the house in a shed the size of a horse stall. It looked like a large doghouse made from sheeting of corrugated steel and wooden boards. Rather hesitantly, she led him inside and closed the door. The tiny room was filled with piles of clothing and her personal belongings. There was a cot and a small table. Looking downcast and embarrassed, Yadira explained that the family who owned the house allowed her to stay without having to pay rent. This was charity. "The family," she explained, "are good people. They are Christians."

For a moment Tommy felt shame. The word *Christian* jolted him like an electric shock. It made him feel guilty—but only for a second. He looked at Yadira and quickly returned to slimy-dog mode. *This is one incredible adventure: a girl who lives in a doghouse! How remarkable!* He embraced Yadira, and told her what a wonderful time he'd had and how lovely she was. "I feel happy again," he said. He made promises he knew he would never keep, that he had no intention of keeping. He returned to the doghouse that afternoon and lavished more attention on her. He bought her presents and told more lies. That night they slept again in his hotel room. More sex. On the second morning, as he walked her home, he promised to arrange for their future together. He said he would be writing soon and that she should remain ready to leave and decide where she wanted to marry.

"I am so happy, Mr. Tommy," Yadira said. "These have been the best two days of my life. I am going to sort through my clothes and start to pack. I will wait for you to write and tell me what to do next. I promise to be ready."

Tommy smiled, but it was all for show. He knew he would never return, never see this girl again. Speedy Gonzales doesn't do second acts. Whatever plans she might make, she would never hear from this prince again.

****

On his drive home, Tommy made a quick stop at Rosario's house. Her son, whose paternity Tommy never acknowledged, was nine years old. After Tommy left Guatemala to attend college, Rosario married Alvaro Gomez, who worked at the mission as a cook and gardener. Seven months later she gave birth to Joshua. Rosario and Alvaro seemed happy together. Even though Rosario discouraged Tommy's attention, he liked to stop by and visit. He assumed Alvaro didn't know that he, Tommy, had fathered Joshua. Rosario acted as if they were casual acquaintances, and they didn't discuss the matter. Tommy didn't bring it up and Rosario never offered information. Tommy had always liked Rosario, just not enough to sacrifice his future for her. Now that she was married and ignored his advances, he found that he was attracted to her even more.

When he reached her house, Rosario was in the kitchen making tortillas. As soon as Tommy realized Alvaro was not at home, he began making jokes and teasing her. He asked her if Joshua was lonely. "Maybe he needs a brother. Maybe he needs someone to play with. Maybe, Rosario, you need someone to play with."

Rosario wasn't amused. "Go home, Tommy. Play with Grace."

Hearing his wife's name brought Tommy back to reality. "How is Joshua?" he asked."

"He is fine," she said, as she swiftly patted out tortillas, slapping the dough from hand to hand. "He is happy and healthy, a good boy. Alvaro and I love him very much."

Tommy understood that mentioning her husband and his love for Joshua was Rosario's way of saying that Joshua was not Tommy's business. It wasn't that Tommy couldn't take a hint, he just didn't want to. For years she had made it clear she wanted nothing to do with Tommy any more. Still, she put up with his teasing and impromptu visits. Tommy assumed it was because she knew he could make things unpleasant for her and Alvaro—not that he ever would. He wasn't that kind of person. Anyway, Tommy didn't want anyone, especially Lester, to know that Joshua was his child.

Rosario continued working on her tortillas as if Tommy wasn't there. She heated the griddle and then neatly spaced the first four tortillas. They were small, and perfectly round, like little saucers. She was totally engrossed in her task, serious and determined. It seemed to Tommy that women after a certain age lost all sense of playfulness; Rosario and Grace were two examples. That's why he preferred younger women. Younger women were more open, and trusting, and fun. They smiled more easily. Rosario seldom smiled at Tommy now. Once she had been a beautiful, fun companion always up for an adventure. Although still attractive, Rosario now acted like a peasant with no aspirations beyond preparing the family meal. He thought of Yadira and the excitement in her eyes the first night they dined in the restaurant. Tommy felt more alive just knowing he was the cause of that excitement. *To hell with Rosario*, he thought. *Stupid Indian.*

Rosario offered Tommy a warm tortilla as it came off the griddle, which he accepted. After wolfing it down, he decided to leave Rosario alone to finish her cooking. But he couldn't resist giving her a good-bye kiss. She stood rigid and unresponsive as he came behind her and gave her a kiss on the back of her neck. Then without a word, he left and headed to his own house.

Tommy wasn't looking forward to arriving home. Seeing Grace only filled him with a sense of emptiness. No matter what he did, Grace managed to make him feel bad about himself. She made it obvious that she didn't desire him, preferring to sleep in a separate bedroom since her last pregnancy. All she ever wanted to talk about, if she could get herself out of bed, was what she called his "character defects." He was sick of being told to pray about his inadequacies. *She should know the half of it*, he thought. Lately she wrote down Bible verses and stuck them on the walls with Scotch tape. Tommy would go in the bathroom to shave and find a verse taped to the mirror. Before leaving on his trip to Minnesota his mirror verse said: *Thou will keep him in perfect peace whose mind is stayed on thee. Isa 26:3*. Grace explained the verses were principles she wanted the family to live by. They made her think positively, she said. But Tommy saw little evidence of a positive effect. Every morning she sat across the table with the same pinched and weary expression, observing him for any tidbit of human frailty that she could pounce upon and dangle before him as evidence of his imperfection. *She needs a saint, not a man. But a saint couldn't pay the bills or keep her in the style to which she is accustomed.* Her hypocrisy irked him, so he shrugged it off. He didn't have time to bother with her attitude. While she was busy pointing her finger and tattling to God, he, Tommy, was actually doing things—important things. He had no intention of taking advice from her on how to be a Christian or a man.

When Tommy arrived home, he was greeted by Evie and Sam. Both were watching a cartoon show on television, but ran up to their father when they saw him in the doorway. They tugged at his pant legs like little monkeys, each trying to be the first to be picked up and held. He picked up Evie first and she planted a big wet kiss on his cheek. Tommy stepped further into the house holding Evie and dragging Sam with his left leg. Then he put Evie down and knelt to give Sam a kiss and hug. Tommy could see that the courtyard was prepared for some type of event, and then he remembered that Thursdays were the Garden Club meetings. Once a month the Garden Club, a group of American women, would meet at one another's house. They were mostly the wives of medical students studying at San Carlos University. A few were wives of businessmen assigned to Guatemala. Aside from being American, they all had two things in common: they were unappealing and they liked to complain about Guatemalans. They seldom talked about gardening. After all, the Guatemalans were the one's who really did most of the gardening.

Tommy headed toward the back of the house so he could shower and change before the Garden Club members arrived. He didn't particularly care for any of the women, but he liked bantering with them. They were hungry for attention and it was fun to flirt. Whenever he walked through during one of their meetings they would call out to him to join them. Then each would try to outdo the other vying for his attention. One had actually propositioned him on the sly—seeking special counseling. He liked to pick out one woman to pay special attention to and let the others smolder. The whole display annoyed Grace, but Tommy found it great fun. However, it never went beyond flirting or the occasional stolen kiss. These pale, civilized women were not to his taste; they reminded him too much of Grace—cold mashed potatoes. He preferred Guatemalan women with blood in their veins instead of embalming fluid. Tommy was sure the Garden Club ladies all considered themselves quite a catch with their neatly coifed hair and matching shoes and purses. They openly disparaged the Guatemalans, complaining that their maids were lazy and unreliable. "They don't take care of their children, and look at the houses they live in." And they made fun of the Guatemalan customs and beliefs. "Can you imagine? My maid tied a lemon slice coated with coffee grounds to her forehead! When I asked why, she said she had a headache." The Garden Club ladies spent a lot of time laughing at the peasants who scrubbed their floors and cooked their food. And Grace was one of the worst complainers. *A fine Christian*, Tommy thought. He found their behavior distasteful and ironic. Not one of the women in the Garden Club could even come close to a Guatemalan in bed. Despite all their superior airs, it wasn't even a close match.

Marta, the nanny, entered the hallway and Tommy handed the children over to her. He asked if Grace was in the back, and Marta nodded and smiled. Tommy asked how Grace was doing. Marta said, "She's not feeling well today, but she is out of bed now. The Garden Club meets today." Then she led the children back to the television.

Tommy headed to the back and knocked once on Grace's door before entering. Grace was sitting at her dressing table brushing her hair and glanced up as Tommy entered the room. Expressionless, she put down the brush and picked up her coffee cup.

"I'm back," Tommy said.

Grace took a sip of coffee. "I expected you two days ago."

"Sorry. I was delayed."

Grace shrugged and replaced the cup. "Business, I'm sure." Tommy noticed a smile (or was it a smirk) ever so slight on Grace's lips. "Are you hungry?" She asked, dutifully. "I'm sure Marta can get you something if you are."

"No," Tommy answered, "I'm fine."

"Well," Grace said, "the ladies are coming." She picked up her brush again and turned toward the mirror. "Maybe later we can talk."

Dismissed, Tommy turned and closed the door. He then headed to his room. His thoughts were again on Yadira and the excitement in her eyes that he had generated. *Maybe I should go back.* If only he could find such excitement with Grace. He entered his room and closed the door. It was then that he noticed the latest Bible verse. It was Scotch taped to his dresser. It said: *For this is the will of God, even your sanctification. That ye should abstain from fornication. 1Th 4:3.*

Jim & Cheryl Pahz

13
TEEN YEARS

It's time for me to confess that I haven't been completely honest. Everything up to this point is true (or at least it could be) according to my inspired recollection of events. But I've left out some stuff about myself. That's because I've done some things I'm not very proud of. Most of my bad behavior was typical teenage fare, but when I look back on it I cringe. I look back a lot.

One of the curses of adoption is that you don't take family for granted. It works both ways, for parents and kids. The parents have to work hard to get their children; they must earn the right to be parents. Then once they receive their child, they constantly question if they are deserving of such a gift, and will they be good enough parents. Adoptive children wonder why they were placed for adoption—really. There's the suspicion that there must be something wrong with them; in some way they are flawed or else why were they given up. Both parent and child live in dread of what will happen when they are exposed for what they secretly fear they might be—a mistake.

Adoptive parents and children love and need one another, but they sometimes question the strength of their claim to one another. Actually, I never questioned my dad's or mom's commitment to me. They demonstrated time after time that I was stuck with them as parents no matter what. Regardless of how poorly I behaved, they loved me and considered me to be a gift they never deserved.

I, on the other hand, did not always appreciate them, and for several years I more resembled a booby prize than the gem they claimed me to be. This only served to infuriate me more. Daniel and Mia so much wanted to be my parents that there seemed to be no challenge they couldn't meet. And believe me; I put them through the ringer.

Things really began to go bad when I was fifteen. That was my stinky year. I was a cheerleader, narcissistic and unpleasant. I was rude and disrespectful to most adults, and I outright lied to my parents. When I was caught, I'd lie some more as well as shout, cry, and slam doors. I became so unruly that I was grounded from cheerleading and taken to a therapist. My official diagnosis was ODD—Oppositional Defiant Disorder—which meant I didn't want to obey rules and I liked to defy authority.

Mia was unimpressed with the diagnosis. She preferred her label: *the stinky child syndrome.* "Isn't this the way all teenagers are?" she asked my therapist, Dr. Goldfeder, who appeared to be on the young side, an impression that was offset by her dark-rimmed glasses and short, sensible haircut. She explained to my mother that it was all a matter of degree. When someone has ODD, the rebellion can be extreme, and the person doesn't respond to the usual forms of discipline. Dr. Goldfeder further explained that my defiance was part of my clinical depression.

My mom could be pretty ODD herself, but she preferred to call it stubbornness and resolve. "What's the difference?" I asked. "You want to get your way, just like me. Why is it that with me it's considered deviant behavior, but with you it's okay?"

"The difference," Mia said, "is that I'm the mom. I'm supposed to get my way. It's my job to tell you what to do. And what I'm telling you is for your own good, even though you can't see it yet."

For years Mom and I clashed. I screamed and shouted. Then I'd stomp up stairs, slam my door and pout. My mom took everything I dished out, like an oak tree standing firm in the middle of a blizzard. Mia was a strong woman. She never knew defeat, only doubt. That was my victory—the doubt that rooted itself in her being and her manner. Doubt seeped into her eyes, her voice and her smile. I discovered doubt is like a stain that can never be completely removed. Lord knows I tried. Once I realized what I'd done, I wanted to undo it. But it was too late. The stain remained. Even though it was just a shadow, it would always be there.

Mia gave me a journal, hoping to inspire me to write. Art had been a refuge for her, and she wanted me to have a safe place of my own to sort out my feelings. I began the journal, just for myself, when I was sixteen, and I've been journal writing ever since. By my senior year of high school my mother and I achieved a truce. I was the hostile one, not Mia. I can't really say why I was so angry, critical, and cruel to my mother; even when I was at my worst I always loved her. And my dad was never really a target unless he sided with Mia against me. Usually our mother/daughter battles were more than he could stomach and, refusing to take sides, he would quietly retreat to their bedroom while Mia and I engaged in combat.

Looking back now, I think of swimming. You know how when you're swimming in a pool and you propel yourself through the water by pushing your legs against the side of the pool? There's a rush of power and freedom as you glide like a bullet before you begin to kick and move your arms. You're not actually trying to push through the wall of the pool; you're just using its strength as a launch pad to see how far you can go. That's what it was like when I fought with Mia. She was the strong wall that I could test my will against. I became so intoxicated with my inflated sense of power, that it took me a long time to realize that she, the wall, was the real source of my strength, and I needed to test my skills outside her safe and secure borders. It was time to leave the swimming pool and head for the ocean. I was seventeen.

Years later I showed my mother one of the entries I had written about our years of turmoil. It was a poem about her and doubt:

My victory is the doubt that will forever
bloom on your face;
The hesitancy in your voice when you
speak my name;
The question in your eyes behind my
reflection;
Your faltering steps as you walk away.

Happiness once so generous and simple –
Like a white tablecloth spread in the
summer sun –
Now marred by the slovenly disregard
of an ungracious guest.
I'm sorry.

Mia smiled and stated that she probably looked better with a little doubt on her face. And regarding the tablecloth, she said that her white tablecloth of happiness was stained long before I came along.

"You really can't know happiness without your tablecloth acquiring a few stains. Thank you," she said, "for your wonderful stains."

14
THE GARDEN

It was Wednesday, February 4, 1976. Grace sat on a bench at the far end of her garden. The children were with Marta and all was quiet except for the chatter of birds and the whispering breeze that fluttered through the flowers. For Grace, the garden was a mystical, healing place. It was one of the few places in the world where she felt she belonged. She would sit in quiet contemplation, gazing at the smiling faces of her favorite flowers. Surrounded by their dazzling silence, she wondered if they, too, were contemplating the world around them.

Tommy avoided the garden, but she wasn't surprised. He had no time for beauty for its own sake. She often thought Tommy had an aversion to the garden—as if it contained something he didn't want to see. *Maybe it's me?* Grace thought. *Probably.*

A poem by Emily Dickinson popped into her head:

Some keep the Sabbath going to church,
I keep it staying at home
With a bobolink for a chorister,
And an orchard for a dome.

Grace had once loved going to church. As a little girl she sat between her parents, dressed in her best clothes, a Sunday visitor to God's house. But when she was in ninth grade her parents were killed in a car accident, and Grace was sent to be raised by her grandparents. After her parents' deaths she clung to church as a way to hold on to them and keep the memory of them alive. She welcomed any insight to heaven, where she was told that her parents had gone. Church became a haven, a spiritual place on earth where anything was possible. God was in His house; even though no one could see Him everybody knew He was there. Perhaps, she had thought, her parents were there, too. She liked to imagine them perched on the ledge of a stained glass window smiling down at her and her grandparents. After the accident, and even before, church provided Grace with a sense of peace and certainty. Now that was gone. Her marriage was a failure, and mission work in Guatemala was not what she expected. It had not brought her closer to God, as she had hoped. If anything, it had distanced her from the Lord.

For the first four years in Guatemala, Grace felt abandoned by God. It was as if a close friend had packed up and moved away, leaving no forwarding address. Grace really didn't blame God. Why would He want to live with her and Tommy? She wasn't even sure she wanted to live with Tommy. Her honeymoon should have been a wake-up call, but Grace was too young and starry-eyed to realize what was happening. She had waited her whole life for the special night when she would give herself to her beloved husband. Her virginity was a gift that she was certain Tommy would appreciate. Instead he acted annoyed by her inexperience. He asked her to do things she didn't understand; things that seemed wrong and unnatural. Too mortified to protest, Grace tried her best to comply, but she felt awkward and stupid.

"Don't you know anything?" Tommy asked, exasperated.

Grace shook her head and burst into tears.

"Okay," he said, trying to sooth her. "We can take care of it. Come here I'll show you."

Grace slid into his arms, grateful to be held and comforted. But once there, Tommy guided her down on the bed and then pounced between her legs. "Relax," he commanded, as he thrust himself forward. Grace tried, but it was painful. She willed herself through the event, wondering if this was what sex was supposed to be like. There must be more, she thought, or why would people like it so much? Eventually Tommy shuddered and then deflated. Then he rested on top of her for a few minutes.

Finally he rolled off and headed for the bathroom. While Tommy was in the bathroom, Grace got out of bed to change the sheets. But there were no other sheets in their hotel room, so she quickly removed the bottom sheet and put the top one on the bottom. When Tommy returned he didn't say anything. He just climbed into bed and fell asleep. Nothing else was said that night. While Tommy slept, Grace was crouched in the bathroom trying to wash the blood out of the sheet. She didn't want the hotel maids to know what happened or to snicker at her behind her back. She felt foolish, cheapened and dirty. Her virginity, which she held in such high regard, was in actuality an embarrassment and most likely a joke for the housekeeping staff. She cried tears of humiliation as she rinsed the blood away.

A few days later, when they were taking an account of their wedding presents, she was dismayed to hear Tommy denouncing those whose present didn't meet his expectations. "What a cheapskate!" He exclaimed. "Look at this! One goblet! Who gives only one goblet?"

"Someone who can't afford two?" Grace offered.

Tommy grimaced and shook his head as he set the offending item aside.

"Honey," Grace gently urged, "that's not the Christian way to accept a gift."

"Maybe," Tommy responded, "but show me where in the Bible it says a Christian is supposed to be cheap."

"Some people can't afford to give more," Grace protested. "Anyway, the important thing is that we're together, not what or how many presents we get."

Tommy seemed unmoved, and continued sorting through the gifts. Eventually he made a list of those he termed *The Cheapos*. Sometimes as Grace reflected in the garden, she wondered what happened to Tommy's list. *It wasn't a list,* she thought. *It was a red flag; a clue that something was seriously wrong. Why didn't I see it?*

After their honeymoon, Grace began seriously praying for Tommy. She still loved her husband, but felt he might need some adjusting. Besides, she had made a vow before God, *for better or worse*. Marriage was sacred and it was forever. "Please, God," she prayed, "speak to his heart. Give him strength and wisdom… give him the desire to be the man he was meant to be." She watched Tommy for any sign of change, but none was apparent. Once they moved to Guatemala, he became even more difficult to understand. When she told him that she was praying for him, he looked annoyed.

"I suppose it can't hurt," he responded. "But

you should also pray for yourself. The problem in this marriage is you." He quoted the Bible, "Wives, submit yourselves unto your own husbands...." Then he would fetch his Bible and turn to the passage in *Ephesians* and continue, "as unto the Lord. For the husband is the head of the wife, even as Christ is the head of the church...therefore, as the church is subject unto Christ, so let the wives be to their own husbands in everything."

This was a passage that Grace would hear over and over in the years ahead, and initially she was astounded and impressed by Tommy's knowledge of the scriptures. When she was alone, she looked up and read the verse that followed aloud to herself. "Husbands love your wives, even as Christ also loved the church, and gave Himself for it." Grace never brought this part of the passage to Tommy's attention. She wasn't really sure if he loved her or not, and she didn't want to make him angry by asking. Besides, she was pregnant.

After the birth of their son, Grace gradually slipped into melancholy. When her daughter, Evie, was born, the depression became worse. Eventually Grace stopped helping out at the mission, and she often stayed in bed for two or three days straight. She lost interest in church, the mission program, her children, everything. Her letters to her grandparents became shorter because there was little to say and she seldom had good news. Besides, she didn't want to burden them with her problems.

How long did this go on for? At least two years, maybe three. Grace wasn't certain of much that occurred during the "dark days," as she called them. The children were cared for by the maid and she thanked Marta for assuming that responsibility. Marta was the one person during this time that she could rely on. Tommy was repulsed by her depression and called her the lump, or lumpfish. Grace ignored him. She was always grateful to see Marta's large round face that reminded her of the moon. Marta had a soft, knowing smile and eyes as calm and deep as a dark lagoon. She was Mayan, and her Indian clothes were cheerfully embroidered with intricate designs.

Marta tried many remedies to raise Grace's spirits—herbal teas, poultices, baths, and incense. Nothing worked. Then one morning she got Grace out of bed and led her zombie-like into the garden. They walked along a pathway around beds of azaleas and hibiscus until they arrived at a hidden spot where Manuel, the gardener, and Marta had set a kitchen chair and a TV table. On the table were coffee, juice, an amazing pastry, and a Bible. Manuel and Marta left Grace alone so the garden (and pastry) could work magic. On that day, alone in the garden, Grace rediscovered her faith and her friend and Lord, Jesus Christ. Once again she felt God's presence, and for the first time in years she smiled.

Gradually the fog lifted and Grace began to heal. She became well enough to get herself out of bed in the mornings, and she took an interest in her house and children. She worked in the garden and attended church. She tried again to become a wife to Tommy, but too much damage had been done.

The kitchen chair and TV table were replaced by sturdier furniture: a wrought-iron patio table and two iron chairs. Although people seldom joined her in the garden, she liked having a second chair for her invisible guest. A stone patio was fashioned underfoot, and was surrounded by flowerbeds that Grace attended to regularly. She worked on the garden continuously to keep the forces of nature at bay. And while she worked on perfecting her flowerbeds, she also worked on examining her life and gaining a sense of meaning and order.

Grace admitted to herself she was not happy, but that was all right. She had given up on happiness and settled for calm. In fact, she preferred her current sense of peace to happiness. Peace was something she could carry within forever; something no one could take away. Happiness depended on others and could easily be lost—just as she had unexpectedly lost her parents, and just as she had lost the love and support of Tommy. That was part of the dilemma she frequently worked on in the garden. What truly had happened to her and Tommy? Who had first lost whom? For a while they had worked together in their marriage; afloat in a hostile sea they had managed for a short time to hold tight to one another as they bobbed above the churning water. But when Grace needed Tommy most, he wasn't there—he let go. In addition to lumpfish, he often called her lazy and reminded her that sloth was one of the seven deadly sins. And wasn't she partially at fault? It was easy to find fault with Tommy; his flaws were obvious for all to see. But in the garden, she came to realize that she had also let him down. She wasn't proud of herself. She had become cranky with everyone, especially the maids. Even Marta, whom she loved dearly, suffered the occasional eruption of Grace's bad temper and ill humor.

The question Grace grappled with was where to go from here. How could she make the best of what was left? They shared two children, and Grace believed Tommy to be a loving, if somewhat inattentive, father. He was a good provider and faithfully sent money to her grandparents each month to help pay expenses now that they were elderly. What did Grace do other than sleep, whine, criticize Tommy, and verbally abuse the maids? She couldn't take care of anyone. Without Marta, she wondered if she could care for herself. All she could do was pull weeds and paste Bible verses on the wall. That was how she communicated with Tommy these days—through pieces of paper on which she scrawled verses meant to pique his interest or direct his efforts. She told herself the verses were to help him become a better person. But deep inside, she knew she pasted them on the walls because Tommy hated it. It was her way to get even.

Did Tommy even read the verses? She doubted it. Once he asked a question about a verse and then never mentioned anything else about them. She guessed that he probably ignored the little pieces of paper, much like he ignored her. And why not? Who was she to give advice? The riddle that Grace needed to solve was not just about Tommy, it was about Grace. Instead of dissecting Tommy's character and whether or not he ever loved her, she had to figure out if she still loved Tommy. She knew she needed him, but did she love him? And if she didn't love him, did she care enough to exert the effort to try and improve the marriage?

One day, kneeling in the flowerbed with trowel in hand, she worked this question in her mind. The garden had taught her an important lesson: miracles happen. All things are possible. Beauty, life, and love are renewable resources that spring forth unexpectedly with amazing speed and strength. In her mind, she traveled back in time to when she first met Tommy, looking for the qualities that attracted her. If she could identify them from her past, perhaps she could rediscover them in the man she was married to.

What she had first noticed about Tommy at Theophilus was that he had a presence about him, and was admired by the other students. He came from a Christian family, and his father was a missionary. Tommy was a basketball player, one of the best on the team, even though a bit on the short side. What he lacked in height he made up for in speed and agility. Grace remembered the incident when Tommy had to make a public apology for attending a movie—a Disney movie for heaven's sake. Grace smiled as she remembered Tommy, defiant but repentant up on the stage. Truth be known, the bad boy image resulting from this episode was one of the things that had attracted her. He had charisma and she saw him as a young Billy Graham—a champion of the Bible. He had the most potential of all of the students she had met at college. At least she thought so at the time.

But Tommy wasn't the only boy at Theophilus interested in Grace. There was Paul Zein from

Nebraska whose parents owned a hog farm. Grace had briefly fantasized about being a farmer's wife, but the thought of the smell of pigs discouraged her. She would always be doing laundry. Anyway, she and Paul had little in common, though he was a cute boy.

Other than Tommy and Paul, the only other boy she had been attracted to was Daniel Fisher, a boy from New York. He was funny and made her laugh, but he wasn't a serious enough Christian for Grace. When Grace first met him, she was sure Daniel wasn't saved, but through lots of hard work she led him to the Lord. That was an accomplishment and she felt like a superhero. His confession of faith, followed by his second baptism, had been a special moment. But Grace always suspected that Daniel was motivated for the wrong reason: not because he desired to be saved, but for her—so she would like him better. She was flattered when he asked her to marry him, but she refused. Although she liked Daniel, they were far too different. She had been raised a Christian, while Daniel was half Jewish without any real religious upbringing. At Theophilus he was reading the Bible for the first time and questioning everything she knew to be true. To Grace, Daniel was more of a pal than a boyfriend. She wished she could have stayed in touch with him, but that wouldn't have been appropriate; especially after she became engaged. Before graduation she gave him a keepsake and sent him on his way. *Daniel was sweet*, she thought.

Grace understood that she was to blame as much as Tommy for the state of their marriage. She was a victim of her own vanity. She had always wanted someone *special*, a man whom others would admire. Tommy certainly fit the bill. Everybody believed Tommy was a cut above the rest. He was good-looking, smart, and athletic. All this and he aspired, as she did, to be a missionary. He even had a program waiting for him in Central America. Tommy was perfect. It all seemed so right in the beginning, that Grace really believed she had been blessed by God. Now she wasn't sure. Was Tommy a blessing or was he instead the mission/challenge God planned for her?

So here she was today, Wednesday, waiting in the garden for her special man to return home. Where was he this time? Or rather, who was it this time? Grace knew Tommy liked women, especially Guatemalan women. No, that wasn't right. Actually, any woman in Central America would qualify. In fact, any woman, anywhere in the world (except for her), could apparently satisfy him. Tommy's only requirement was that the person have a vagina, and once even that requirement was waived. Several years ago Tommy shared a funny story with Grace. As usual he blamed someone else for his own misbehavior, but Grace didn't realize it at the time. According to Tommy, he and his friend Mark (another student from Theophilus) went to Chattanooga during spring break. One night, while driving around, they headed downtown to Ninth Street where they met a prostitute. Ninth Street was a scary place at night, and Tommy was nervous. The prostitute invited them both up to her apartment for a "date." Mark decided to go, but Tommy was too leery—he stayed in the car with the motor running, just in case they needed to make a quick exit. They did. Five minutes later, Mark jumped in the car, too panicked to even breathe right. As Tommy sped off, Mark described through gasping breaths that he had placed his hands between the woman's legs only to discover that she was really a man. "Can you believe it?" Tommy laughed.

Grace saw the humor but she was concerned. "Why were you looking for prostitutes," she asked, "when you're a Christian?"

"I wasn't," Tommy assured her. "Mark was. He's always doing stuff like that."

A few years later Mark and his wife, Karen, visited Grace and Tommy in Guatemala. One night while the men were out, Grace and Karen had a heart-to-heart talk about husbands and marriage. They were living dangerously that night, and had a little wine with their chips and pretzels. Eventually the conversation veered from trivial complaints to more intimate concerns. Grace was in good spirits and relished the chance to discuss some of the nitty-gritty details of married life with another young American woman. Then she stepped on a land mine. She shared the story of Mark and Tommy's great adventure on Ninth Street. As the story unfolded, Karen listened intently with a queer expression on her face. Grace ended by stating, "You must have your hands full with Mark, what with his need for sexual adventure."

To her surprise, Karen burst into laughter. "I don't know, Grace. You tell me," and then Karen howled even more, spilling wine on her white T-shirt.

Grace watched as Karen kicked her feet back and forth, hysterical with laughter. *Is it the wine?* Grace wondered, feeling the urge to laugh, too. *Is she intoxicated?*

Karen finally settled down, and wiped tears from the corner of her eyes. She took a deep breath.

Then she said, with as serious a face as she could muster, "Really, you can't possibly believe it was Mark who went with the prostitute!"

"What... what do you mean?" stammered Grace.

"Grace," Karen looked at her quizzically, "it

was Tommy who went, not Mark. Mark's way too much of a coward for something like that. He'd be too scared to even talk to a prostitute."

"But Tommy said...."

Karen shook her head and set her wine glass on the coffee table. Then she leaned forward and took Grace's hand. "I don't know what Tommy said, but I know for a fact it was Mark who waited in the car. Mark tells me everything he ever did, which really isn't much compared with Tommy."

Karen gently squeezed Grace's hand and looked at her with sympathy. "Mark doesn't lie to me, Grace. There's no need to. I might not like what he says, but I accept it. And anyway, I don't care what he did before we were married. But to tell the truth, even if he saw a prostitute today, he'd probably tell me. That's Mark and that's the way I want him to be. I'd rather hear the truth than be told a lie. I don't want everyone else talking about things I don't even know about behind my back. The fact of the matter is that Tommy is dick-driven. That's how Mark puts it. Where it leads, Tommy will follow."

"Where what leads?" Grace stammered. She was beginning to feel light-headed.

"Mr. Johnson... his member. You know, his penis!"

As Grace listened, she knew in her heart

Karen was telling the truth. Of course it was Tommy who went with the prostitute. It was Tommy who lied. It was always Tommy—her husband. How could she have been so naïve to think otherwise?

The incident with Tommy and the prostitute was just another crack in Grace's fantasy picture of Tommy and her marriage. Since their wedding night there had been so many cracks that by now the image resembled a shattered mirror. The latest cracks were caused by rumors about Tommy's activities with various women. She heard it whispered that the son of Rosario, a woman who worked in the mission office, looked a lot like Tommy. She wasn't going to think about Rosario. It was a waste of time and it was painful. But if true, that meant that years before their marriage, Tommy was behaving badly. Rosario's son was at least nine or ten years old.

Sadly, Grace concluded Tommy was never the man she had thought he was. *Tommy isn't special,* she thought, jabbing the ground with her trowel. *He's ordinary. Who cares who he sleeps with? He's less than ordinary; he's common. And I married him. So what does that make me?*

Grace felt tears running down her face. Where was her husband now? Would Tommy be home tonight, and, if so, would they fight again? When they were in college they had argued a lot and it was fun, a game. But it wasn't amusing anymore. So much had changed.

Grace sat still, her legs folded under her feeling the moist warmth of the soil. *God, why have you abandoned me? Is it because I married Tommy? Is it because I've become a lumpfish?*

She closed her eyes and softly prayed, "Oh, Jesus, gracious Lord and Savior, remember me? I need help. My marriage is terrible, and I can't seem to make it better. My whole life is out of control. Are you testing me, Lord? I know I've made bad choices. I'm weak and I don't understand what I need to do. Please, Lord, help me out of this wilderness. Speak to me, Lord, and show me the way. Please, God, hear my prayer. In Jesus' name I pray. Amen." She paused and wiped the tears on her face with the back of her hands.

Then she felt the ground beneath her quiver. It was as if the earth was inhaling—taking a deep breath. Her whole body sensed a vibration, ever so slight. Grace wasn't sure what had happened, but she felt momentarily disoriented. Grace opened her eyes and slowly looked around, as if seeing the world for the first time. Everything appeared crystal clear with nothing obviously amiss. The flowers swayed gracefully and the yellow trowel was still in her hand. Yet something was very different. Grace thought, *God has not abandoned me. He has answered my prayer.* She bowed her head and closed her eyes, whispering, "Thank you, Lord. Thank you."

Jim & Cheryl Pahz

15
CHRYSALLIS

The 1976 earthquake in Guatemala killed more than 22,000 people and injured over three times that many. For Grace the earthquake was a turning point. It was the miracle through which God reentered her life. She was in her garden, asking God to help with her marriage, and suddenly God answered. She didn't hear actual words or see a burning bush, but as she knelt in the dirt with tears streaming down her face, she felt the earth breathe beneath her. It was ever so slight and yet quite clearly perceptible. Alarmed, she opened her eyes and found God all around her—He smiled at her through the flowers swooning in the sunshine; He called to her from the sky through the voices of birds that sang His praises. She felt Him in the breeze that caressed her skin. So clear was His presence, it was like a light switch had been turned on in her head.

When she later heard about the earthquake on the news, logic told her the movement she felt in the garden was simply the earth shifting during the terrible event. Canoguitas was far away from the epicenter. What had she felt? Was it the earthquake or an aftershock? She didn't know, but she realized God would not cause such a terrible event simply to have a conversation with her about her broken marriage. *How could I possibly be so foolish and self-absorbed?* Grace was shamed by her vanity. And yet she could not dismiss the notion that God truly had been present with her in the garden and had spoken to her. Somehow she and the earthquake were linked in an important and yet undetermined way. Grace told no one what happened in the garden. It was a secret between her and her Lord. She quietly accepted it all on faith, and patiently waited for God's plan to unfold before her.

Grace did not have to wait long. After the earthquake, life was so chaotic that travel and other hallmarks of normal routines vanished. Over a million people were homeless and in desperate need of help. Three days after the disaster, a village woman brought Joshua Gomez to Grace's house. All the homes in the countryside were overrun with survivors from the city returning. Remnants of families were being crudely patched back together as each took stock of the toll the earthquake had wrought in their lives. At the time of the earthquake, Joshua had been in school, and his parents, Rosario and Alvaro, were shopping in Guatemala City. After the earthquake they did not return home, and there were no other relatives to be found to care for the boy.

Grace took Joshua into her home for safekeeping until his parents came for him. But more days passed, and still they did not return. *Perhaps,* Grace had thought, *Rosario and Alvaro are injured and languishing in one of the makeshift hospitals. Maybe they are dead. No.* Grace refused to accept that thought. *Rosario and Alvaro are strong. They must be working with the Red Cross or some other emergency relief effort.* But Grace knew this was a long shot. *Two loving parents would not leave their child unattended in an emergency, would they?* The answer was simple: *Of course not.*

Grace had never liked Rosario. She believed the woman flaunted her beauty to attract attention. She was also concerned because Rosario was outspoken regarding her political views. Grace felt it might jeopardize the ministry, and she had cautioned Tommy about this possibility.

"Rosario praises the insurgents," Grace warned Tommy. "She calls them resistance fighters. I've heard her support goes beyond words. This could make her and her family a target, and I'm afraid this might cast suspicion on the mission. It might be wise to terminate her employment."

Tommy's response was devoid of any respect for Grace's observations. "Are you sure it's Rosario's politics that concerns you, or is it her looks? Anyway, what would a lumpfish know of politics?" He laughed. "When exactly did this insight come to you? While you were lying in bed?"

Grace didn't let her suspicions about Rosario color her feelings for Joshua. He was, after all, an innocent child... a victim. He arrived on her doorstep a quiet, serious boy who appeared mature beyond his ten years of age. Even though he was famished, he ate the food Grace offered slowly, with dignity. After dinner he took a bath with Sam, and Grace gave him one of Tommy's clean T-shirts to sleep in. The plastic sack he arrived with contained only a change of underwear, some socks, a Bible, and a photograph of his parents holding him when he was a baby. Before bed that first night, Sam and Evie scrambled into Grace's room to hear a bedtime story. Josh followed, shy and uncertain what to do. He sat down quietly beside Grace while she read *Where The Wild Things Are* by Maurice Sendak. Afterward, while Sam and Evie bounced on the bed and squealed, Josh examined the storybook— intently studying each page as if the pictures held answers to questions he didn't know how to ask. That night Josh slept on a cot in Sam's room, and he was still holding the book when Grace turned out the light.

"Put the book down sweetie and try and get some sleep. We can read it again in the morning."

Weeks turned into months, and still there was

no word of Rosario or Alvaro. The cot in Sam's room was replaced by a new twin bed, and dark thoughts entered Grace's mind. *Rosario and Alvaro are not coming home.* Whether it was the earthquake that had swallowed them up or something else, she would never know. But they were gone, and somebody needed to care for Joshua. Grace knew she was that somebody. She and Joshua were linked for all time by the earthquake and by God.

Each night before going to sleep, Joshua would ask Grace the same questions: "When will my parents come home?"

Grace smiled and said, "When God wills it."

"But, will I ever see them again?"

"Yes, if God wills it."

"But when?"

"When the time is right. Only God knows that time. Now, sleep (or eat, or do your homework) and be strong. Be a good son for them… and for us, too. And remember, Joshua, God has a plan for your life."

After a year, the questions diminished and then stopped. Joshua grew up with Sam and Evie. He played with them and eventually merged into their family. He called Grace and Tommy "Mom" and "Dad," just as Sam and Evie did. And as Grace had requested, he had become a good son. Over time he became her special boy. Grace loved

Joshua as her own child, and she could not imagine life without him. Two years after his arrival, the Tuttles formally adopted him.

But to Grace, Joshua was more than a son. He was the answer to her prayers. Joshua was the beacon that guided Grace on the path God meant for her to follow. She had clearly seen the path on the day of the earthquake; it was Joshua who showed her how to walk it.

First, she realized she must stop whining and climb out of her depression. She must resolutely take up her cross and follow Jesus, as the Lord commanded the disciples in the *Book of Matthew*. Grace wasn't exactly sure what her cross was, but she suspected her husband Tommy had more than a little to do with it. She would follow her destiny wherever it would lead. I *want my life to be a testimony to Christ. I want people to see the Lord living in me.* To do this she must stop regarding her husband and her marriage as burdens; instead, her circumstances should be considered challenges and a test of her faith. She would accept them as gifts, learning opportunities from which she would become strengthened. It was not a matter of success or failure; it was acceptance with courage and faith that were important.

Grace continued to read her Bible, but now it was less for instruction and more for the sense of closeness to God. The Bible was no longer a collection of puzzles to be deciphered and memorized; it wasn't instructions for her husband.

She now read the Bible for inspiration. She continued to copy verses and tape them to her doors and walls, but now she did it for herself. The scriptures were buoys to help mark her passage through turbulent waters. It was no longer her job to correct others, including Tommy. She would leave that task to God, whom she trusted to act on Tommy in His own way and in His own time. She would concentrate on Grace. She would try to be a better person, and an example to others.

At first it was difficult for Grace because she had become a sour woman. But with the Lord's help, she knew change was possible. *All things are possible to those who love the Lord. I do.* She began by vowing to perform one act of kindness each day, and she worked hard to honor this promise. Everyday she drew inspiration from Joshua. She was continually awed by the power of his calm and quiet patience, and his simple acceptance of events he could not understand. She came to believe that God sent Joshua for a reason and that reason was to lead her out of whatever darkness remained in her life, "… *and a little child shall lead them.*" She contemplated the words of the prophet Isaiah, and reflected on the role of Joshua in her life.

Eventually Grace withdrew from the garden club (which didn't really have much to do with gardening) and began doing volunteer work, above the little bit of work she did for the Evangelical Friendship Mission of Guatemala. She worked with all organizations that had churches or programs in Canoguitas, including the Catholics, Mormons, and Jehovah's Witnesses. Work on behalf of others brought her contentment, and she found that when she was thinking of others, she had little time to brood about herself. She particularly liked working with Father Martin, whom she found to be a highly intelligent and spiritual man.

The maids and household workers immediately noticed the difference in Grace. For so long the house had been under a cloud; now the sun was breaking through. Grace enjoyed the smiles that greeted her each day, and the quiet songs and gentle laughter that drifted through the rooms and mingled with the sounds of people at work. She began to be a real mother again—enjoying all three children and taking pleasure in the simple chores of motherhood. *There is nothing like the laughter of children,* she thought. *It lifts my spirits to the very threshold of heaven.*

People within her church community didn't know what to think of the "new" Grace. Some expressed concern to Tommy because her

Catholic neighbors suggested she might be a saint, like Brother Peter of Antigua. Tommy scoffed at such an idea—he didn't believe in saints and he disapproved of Grace's ecumenicalism. He suggested Grace restrict her work to the activities of the mission. Some of the congregation referred to their Catholic neighbors derogatorily as "Papists," and argued that Grace shouldn't assist them because they weren't really Christians.

Grace ignored such advice. "Nonsense!" she exclaimed. "Of course they are Christians. They have Christ in their hearts—that's what makes a Christian. Look at all the good Father Martin does." Then she would turn the table on her critic and ask, "How long has it been since you distributed food to the poor?" Her point was made.

After Joshua came, Grace began to notice a gradual change in Tommy's attitude toward her. The sarcastic names and insulting remarks diminished, and she began to detect something akin to respect. Although they still had little in common, they were at least civil to one another. The children offered a neutral ground, or safe zone, for Grace and Tommy's troubled relationship. They shared their meals with the children, and most of their private conversations revolved around one or more of the children—which one needed a trip to the city, who was doing poorly in studies, or who wanted a larger allowance. When Grace and Tommy appeared together in public, it was as a family with the children between them. They looked at, spoke, and touched one another through their children. It was a lonely marriage between two people separated by an ocean of lies and broken promises. The children were a bridge where the couple could sometimes meet, if only for a short time.

The one place where Grace and Tommy did not meet was in the bedroom. They each had their own room. Tommy was free to come and go as he pleased while Grace settled into a small room close to the children. In this manner, time passed and the months turned into years and the children grew. Each of her children brought her a special joy. Each was unique. At eighteen, Josh had become an especially handsome young man who stood tall and straight with wavy black hair and intense brown eyes. He remained serious and quiet, like the boy on that first night, but not in a cold or aloof way. He was sensitive and thoughtful, and despite his good looks, he was always polite and helpful—especially to Grace. Sometimes Tommy suggested that Grace favored Josh and gave him more attention than the others. But Grace knew that wasn't so. She loved all her children equally and they each filled her heart with joy. Evie and Sam were children of her body; Josh was the child of her soul.

16
EASTER WEEK

I was sixteen years old when I took my first trip to Guatemala. I was in the middle of my stinky period, and my parents thought the trip might help. They were desperate and willing to try almost anything. But I was such a brat that nothing could have helped. The trip only provided me with new territory for my performances along with numerous opportunities to aggravate my parents. I doubt they guessed that behind my sullen exterior I was actually enjoying myself. How could they guess? I didn't even realize it at the time. The fact is, my memories from that first Guatemala trip are some of the happiest I have, and I have a lot of happy memories.

The first two days we stayed at the Hotel Pan American in downtown Guatemala City. I immediately balked because it was not the luxurious accommodations I was expecting. The streets in the city were narrow and crowded and there was a grimy smell that stuck to your skin. The hotel was ancient with rickety elevators and sparse rooms. When we first entered the lobby, I thought of the movie *Casablanca*, but instead of Bergman and Bogart, the place was abuzz with a cast of characters who looked remarkably like me—small and dark. Suddenly I was in a world where the majority of residents had black hair and skin in various shades of coffee, from café con léche (like mine) to dark espresso.

"See!" my father announced excitedly, "the staff all wear traditional Mayan clothing. The material is handwoven and each village has its own unique pattern." He was proud to share this information, even though he and mom had already told me this a hundred times. But now he offered proof.

My response was tepid. "Gee whiz Dad, can you please keep it down? You're embarrassing me."

Once in our room, I plopped on one of the uncomfortable beds and looked around. There was a workable television, but when I turned it on the only English programs were quiz shows or old reruns of *Bonanza* and *Gunsmoke*. I fell backward on the bed feeling sorry for myself. "It's not fair. This is supposed to be a vacation. Why do we have to stay in this run-down hotel?"

One thing I will give the hotel credit for was the food. It was delicious. Naturally I complained because I couldn't find my favorites on the menu. Instead of bagels and cream cheese for breakfast we had *huevos rancheros* (scrambled eggs with salsa) and a platter of colorful fruits. I can't name all of the fruits I ate during the trip, but they were all delicious. I quickly learned the name for French fries *(papas fritas)* and this became my favorite snack. They tasted different from the American version, but just as good—maybe a little better and the catsup was sweeter. Throughout the day, musicians played folk music and, despite myself, I liked the place. It was both comic and exotic, and each time I entered the lobby was like stepping into a movie.

We did a lot of walking in Guatemala City and went to some museums and a municipal zoo. Many shops sold antiquities such as old jewelry, Spanish doubloons, antique statues, and pottery. In one shop I found a hand-carved wooden box about the size of two shoeboxes side by side. The carving on the top of the box, intricate and delicate, depicted a quetzal bird perched amidst a forest. Other smaller birds were captured in flight in the carved border around the sides of the box. I was mesmerized and irrationally certain that this particular box had been sitting right here in Guatemala City for sixteen years just waiting for me to come in and get it. My parents bought the box, and as I carried it back to the hotel, I knew I'd found a treasure.

On the third morning, we left for Antigua, which Mom and Dad claimed would be the highlight of the trip. They had made reservations almost a year in advance because Antigua is so crowded during Semana Santa, Holy Week. My mother was raised by a Jewish mother and Catholic father. Somehow she was able to join both religions in a way that worked, and her Catholic part was very excited about this event. "People come here from all over the world," she said. "It's said to be one of the most beautiful and moving religious ceremonies in the Americas. And imagine, it's been going on since the fifteen hundreds!"

I was excited, but for a different reason. Our accommodations in Antigua were far move luxurious and resort-like than the Pan American Hotel. In Antigua our place had a beautiful courtyard with gardens and a swimming pool where I could bask in my new swimsuit and watch the colorful parrots perched in the trees. Of course I'd have to make a few obligatory appearances to the main events, but I was confident I could keep my involvement with Mom's religious agenda to a minimum. Any activity that involved walking, I could whine my way out of by claiming my feet hurt or threatening an asthma attack.

The celebration began on Ash Wednesday, the first day of Lent, and climaxed with a spectacular procession through the town streets on Good Friday. The streets were covered with intricate designs made out of colored sawdust. The colorful sawdust cushioned the feet of the believers who would walk over them carrying statues of Christ and various saints. The beautiful sawdust-art took days to create, only to be destroyed as it was trampled by the procession. We staked our spot along one of the crowded streets and watched as the parade of believers dressed in costumes walked through the sawdust. Some of the participants were dressed like priests and swung balls of incense that filled the air with a smoky haze that smelled acrid and unpleasant. This was the excuse I was looking for. "Mom! I need to go back and get my inhaler or I'm going to start coughing and wheezing."

But my mother had anticipated this move. "I've got your inhaler," she said, producing it from her shirt pocket.

I took a couple of puffs. "I think I'm going to need a vaporizer. There's too much smoke here."

She nodded and pulled me back into the crowd. "We'll move away from the smoke," she said and my dad led us back a few feet and into an alcove that was really the entrance to a building where we could stand on some steps and watch the procession more comfortably. I watched as a group of women dressed in black approached, carrying a statue of the Virgin Mary. As I looked into their faces, it occurred to me that one of them could be my birth mother.

Was Felicita here among these people? Would she be carrying the Virgin Mary as an act of adulation or as an act of penance for giving me up for adoption? Maybe I had a brother or sister passing before me in the procession. I remembered Felicita's recipe book, filled with her spells, poems, and recipes. Suddenly I wanted to be able to read them. I wanted to know if her magic worked. Could I alter my life by reading her words? I gazed at the crowd. Wasn't this whole celebration a sort of magic ceremony? Didn't these pilgrims believe, by honoring their deities, their lives would improve? And isn't that what Felicita's spells were all about— making life better? Then I realized that Mia and Felicita, two women born worlds apart, might not be so different after all.

Following the procession, we walked back to the hotel as the sawdust was being swept from the streets. We rested a couple of days and then rented a car and driver to take us to the Department of Esquintla. We were going to a village named Canoguitas to visit the Evangelical Friendship Mission of Guatemala. This was my beginning. It was the place where, as Mom put it, "the miracle happened."

17
FELICITA

Grace was trimming the large clusters of purple flowers from her big heads plant *(Cattleya skinneri)* in her front yard when she noticed a young woman walking toward her down the street which had no name. The woman was small in stature with fine features, and waddled like a duck as she approached the walkway to the house. She was carrying a small bundle and a black notebook in one hand. The other arm was hugging her large belly as she walked, as if supporting a basket of laundry. *She must be due any day,* Grace thought as she laid the pruning shears on the ground. She swiped a stray strand of hair from her eyes and watched the woman approach. The woman, Grace saw, was actually quite young—a girl perhaps three or four years older than Evie. She was pretty, but appeared weary and unkempt. The clothes she wore were tattered, and her shoes so badly worn that they were coming apart. Grace sensed that the girl's weariness came from within, rather than from the exertion of walking, as if the young woman had seen or done too much in her short lifetime. Grace thought, *whoever she is, I know her weariness.*

The girl stopped a few yards from Grace. "May I offer you my salutation?" she asked. "I search for man who is reverend here." She spoke in broken English, looking sadly at Grace. Her dust-covered cheeks were streaked, and Grace couldn't tell if it was from sweat or tears.

"Reverend Tuttle is probably in the administration building," Grace replied and pointed toward the compound.

"I come from there. I don't mean old man. I mean young old man."

Grace was puzzled. There was only one minister in the compound, but there were two men named Tuttle.

"His name is Thomas," the woman continued, "like in Bible; man who doubts Lord Jesus."

"Oh, you must mean Tommy." Grace could see the girl was struggling with English, so she continued in Spanish. "Tommy is not here now. Is there something I can do for you?"

The girl paused for a moment as if to size up the situation. "Well," she continued, "I am hungry. I haven't eaten for a long time." She looked relieved to speak in her native tongue. "I am worried about the baby. If the mother does not eat properly, will that not hurt the baby?"

"Yes, I suppose it can," Grace answered. "When are you due?"

"Soon. I am not sure exactly, but I think my baby will come soon."

"What is your name?" Grace asked.

"Felicita Rodriguez."

"Why did you come here, Felicita? Why did you come to this place?"

"To see the Reverend Thomas. I was told to come here because the Reverend Thomas can help me." She paused and turned her gaze downward toward the ground. "My father made me leave. He said that we could not support another mouth to feed. He said my pregnancy is shameful. I have nowhere else to go. People told me about the Friendship Mission and that Reverend Thomas could help me."

"Who told you?"

"People. I do not remember who they are."

"What about your baby's father? Where is he?"

"He left. I do not know where he is. I do not even know who he is. I met him once; only one time. He is unknown."

Unknown? Grace thought. *What a strange thing to say. How can you not know who your baby's father is? Has someone coached her to use that word? Maybe a lawyer? Maybe....* "Where do you come from, Felicita? Where is your home?"

"Mazatenango."

Mazatenango was about four hours by car from Canoguitas—a long way to come.

Grace rose to her feet and removed her gardening gloves. Then she smiled at Felicita and extended her hand. "Please, come into my house. I will have Marta prepare us something to eat. We can wait together. My husband will be home soon, but I think you should know he's not a minister; he's a program director. You should not call him reverend. Most people just call him Tommy."

****

When Tommy arrived in the late afternoon, Grace and Felicita were resting in the courtyard. Felicita was stretched in a lounge chair sipping lemonade. As soon as Tommy walked through the entrance, Felicita sat up. Although she was eager to see Tommy, she now appeared uncomfortable and hung her head to avoid eye contact.

"I was told you could help me," she said. "I am going to have a baby."

"I believe the ministry can find a family for your child," Tommy responded. "If that's what you want."

"Yes, Reverend, because I cannot keep this baby."

Grace sat passively observing. She had a nagging feeling that something was going on beneath the surface. *Has he seen this woman before? Could Tommy have been the one to coach her? This is the third baby in six months to find its way to the ministry.* Grace had learned of the other two children through one of her maids. *What happened to those babies? Were there others?* As Tommy spoke to Felicita, Grace listened with interest and said nothing.

Tommy sat down across from Felicita. The young girl remained rigid with her eyes downcast as Tommy spoke. Grace was surprised by the patience and concern Tommy showed towards the young woman.

"This is an important decision, Felicita," he said. "Why don't you rest now? You can sleep in a guesthouse and we can talk more tomorrow."

Felicita nodded, and Grace noticed a small tear slide down the side of her face. It left a glistening scar. Slowly, Felicita rose from her seat. She smiled shyly as she said goodnight to Grace, and then turned to follow Marta and Tommy to one of the guest cottages. Grace remained in the courtyard. She wanted to give this matter some thought, and most of all, she needed to pray.

****

During the next few weeks, Grace observed Felicita waddle around the compound carrying her black notebook. The two women often shared lemonade in the afternoon. Felicita spoke of her unborn baby with affection, and Grace wondered if she would really release the child for adoption after it was born. When the time came, could Felicita let go of the child she so obviously loved?

"I am sure it will be a girl," Felicita said. "We have many girls in our family." Her smile was broader these days and her skin glowed. Rested and cleaned, she hardly looked like the same girl who only weeks earlier had wandered into the compound. Grace was struck by Felicita's natural beauty and gentle nature. Felicita reminded her of a wildflower.

"With you as her mother, she will be a beautiful child," Grace said. "I'm sure of that."

Felicita smiled, but Grace sensed her unspoken sadness. She didn't push, but she did pray for Felicita as she worked in her garden each day. The baby was born at 2:00 in the morning. It was a girl, just as Felicita had predicted. When the doctor arrived, he pronounced her healthy. The baby was kept in a separate room from Felicita, because she wasn't sure about seeing her baby. But Grace checked on the little girl, and held her in her arms. She was beautiful and petite, just like her mother. "I knew it," Grace said. "Just like I thought."

Then Grace went to Felicita and sat by her side as she slept. When Felicita awoke, the first thing she asked was: "Did you see her? Did you see my baby?"

"Of course. She is beautiful, just like you. And she has all ten fingers and toes. In fact, she is as close to a perfect baby as any I have ever seen."

Felicita smiled contentedly.

"Do you want to hold her?" Grace asked.

Felicita shook her head. "No. It is best I do not. Mr. Tommy says it is a bad idea. I just want her to have a good family and a better life. I want good parents who will love her. Someone like you."

Grace smiled and embraced Felicita. The two women cried.

The next afternoon, when Grace arrived for a visit, both Felicita and the baby were gone. All that was left was Felicita's black notebook lying conspicuously on the table by her bedside.

Grace felt a profound emptiness. No one had any answers for her, and she was on the verge of panic when she confronted Tommy.

"What happened?" she asked. "Where is Felicita?"

"I don't know," Tommy shrugged. "She left."

"What do you mean, she left?"

"She left. What's not to understand?"

"Did she walk? Did you drive her? Did she

take a bus?"

"I don't know. I didn't drive her. I guess she got a ride."

"And the baby?"

"The baby's fine," Tommy said. "Don't worry."

"But where is the baby?"

"In foster care."

"What foster care? Since when does the mission have foster care?"

Tommy gave her a harsh look—the one he used with employees who overstepped their boundaries or the children when they misbehaved. "Stop questioning me, woman," he said, clearly irritated. "I'm doing my job." Then he walked away.

****

Grace was beside herself. She needed to see for herself what had become of Felicita's baby, but to do so she needed to find the so-called foster care. Early the next morning she paid Lester a visit. His appearance startled her and she tried to remember just how old Lester was. Grace realized, guiltily, that it had been several weeks since she had even spoken with him. He looked old—older than usual. She noted his pale and frail appearance and decided she must mention to Tommy how poorly he looked.

Lester acted confused, as if he had been drinking, but Grace knew he didn't drink. He was also evasive and reluctant to reveal any information. Still, she pressed him and eventually she learned the mission had rented a house in the Rapado, a small cluster of buildings about eight miles away.

Lester's directions were sketchy, but with enough solid detail that Grace was confident she could locate the house. He said the house was painted green and stood behind a milpah, a patch of corn. The house was supposed to be surrounded by a circle of rocks. The rocks were painted white and Lester said there was a red and yellow hammock on the porch.

It took Grace almost two hours to locate the property. Lester forgot to mention that behind the cornfield was a grove of trees, and the house was nestled deeply within the grove. She was about to give up the search, assuming that Lester was as confused as he appeared, when she decided to follow the two-track road that ran along the north side of an overgrown patch of what looked like an abandoned cornfield. As she came to the end of the corn, she caught a glimpse of the white stones and the house hidden within the trees. There was indeed a red and yellow hammock on the porch, just as Lester described. She stopped the car at the edge of the trees and cautiously walked up the path. As she approached, she heard a baby whimpering and she quickened her pace. Without stopping to knock, she pulled open the screened door and entered, following the sounds she assumed were from Felicita's baby.

Once inside the house, she was overwhelmed by the heat and then the stench of urine. She was vaguely aware of the sound of flies buzzing from somewhere, and she had to remind herself to breathe. While her eyes adjusted to the dark interior, she put her hand over her nose and mouth and slowly proceeded into a room where she found three toddlers sharing a crib. One was the source of the whimpering she had heard, and the other two immediately began to howl when they saw her. Grace's eyes moved to a second crib where she saw two infants. One looked to be a few months old and the other was a newborn. Grace felt her heart jump—Felicita's baby! Without thinking, she charged toward the crib and scooped the baby into her arms. *Who could leave a baby in place like this?* "My goodness gracious," Grace murmured as tears welled in her eyes. She clutched the infant and then stood stunned, gazing at the other children. "What's to be done? I can't hold you all." In an instant her sadness gave away to anger. "Hello!"

She shouted, turning around. "Is anybody here?"

She heard a moan from an adjacent room and a young woman appeared in the doorway. She wore a stained, once-white cotton dress and a pair of blue flip-flops. The woman looked to have just been awakened. Her hair was uncombed and she had a wild appearance about her. She leaned against the doorway unconcerned as she beheld Grace holding the baby.

"Who are you?" Grace demanded in Spanish.

The woman shrugged, "I was resting. The heat is terrible." Quick as a lizard, she grabbed a fly from the air and crushed it in her fist. Then she slowly opened her hand to confirm her victory. She smiled and flicked the insect to the floor. "What do you mean, who am I? Who are you? Are you the mother?" She looked at Grace with tired, indifferent eyes.

"Of course not!" Grace snapped. Several flies were circling her head, and Grace waved her hand over the baby's face to shoo them away. "Who do these children belong to?" Grace demanded.

"You don't know?" the woman replied sullenly.

Grace was livid. She completely forgot about her one-act-of-kindness rule and snapped. "Who's in charge here?" She was in no mood for the woman's insolence.

"Señor Tommy pays me my money. He is the boss."

Grace noted the confident smirk on the woman's face. *I might have known,* she thought. "This child is ill," she said, moving with the baby toward the door. "I am taking her home with me."

"Oh, no. No. You cannot do that." The woman was suddenly alert, wide-eyed and defiant. "Señor Tommy says nobody is supposed to come here. Nobody has anything to do with the children. It is a private matter. That is what he says."

"Well, I don't care what Señor Tommy says. I am Señora Tommy. Do you understand? I am the wife and I am taking this baby home with me right now. She needs a doctor. Do you understand or are you just too ignorant to notice that this baby is sick?"

"Sí, señora, I understand."

Grace peered hard at the woman, staring her down. "I will return tomorrow, and when I do I want this place clean. I want clean diapers on these children. I want the food cleared from the table, and I want this terrible smell and the flies gone. Señor Tommy pays you to do a job. He will be angry if I tell him what I found here today. Do I make myself clear?"

"Sí, señora. Whatever you say, I will do."

Grace could see now the woman was clearly

concerned. This job was probably the only source of income for an entire family.

"Take care of these things by tomorrow. If you do as I say, you'll still have a position here; if you don't, you will have to answer to me. Not answer to Señor Tommy, but to me." Then she walked out of the house, carrying the baby to her car.

When she reached the car she was trembling. Tears rolled down her cheeks. She closed her eyes and prayed: "Forgive me, Lord, for losing my temper. I am sorry, God, but this baby is so helpless... so innocent. And Lord, I love this baby. This is Felicita's baby. Forgive me, God, I am weak. I mistreated that woman. I lost control and I lied about the baby being sick. I am sorry, Lord, but this baby is special... forgive me."

****

Later that evening, when Grace confronted Tommy, he was not pleased.

"Ten thousand dollars, Grace! That's our portion for an adoption. I mean the ministry's portion. It covers all the expenses—the medical, the foster care, and the birth mother's expenses. It doesn't include lawyers' fees. The families pay extra for that. We need this money, Grace. The mission needs the money."

Grace looked at her husband. "And the baby? Does she have a family?"

He shook his head. "Not Felicita's baby. Not yet. It's too soon. We don't have her paperwork."

"Have you been inside that house? Have you seen how the babies are kept?"

Tommy didn't answer.

"It's inhumane. It's dangerous, Tommy. And it's certainly not Christian. Those babies could get sick, or even die in conditions like that."

"I'm sorry, Grace. I didn't realize. I'll check it out tomorrow. I promise."

"No, Tommy, I'll do it. I want to go back and see for myself. I told your worker she would have to answer to me."

He looked surprised, "Why?"

"Because those babies need me. They need someone who cares. You say that the ministry needs this. Well, then, I want to help. This is something I can do. If you promise that these children truly need to be adopted, then I can assist and help keep them safe. Except..." She paused.

"Except...what? What's the catch?"

"Except not Felicita's baby."

"We can't place it for adoption?" He whined, clearly wounded by the request.

"I didn't say that."

"It's a lot of money. Lester will not be pleased," Tommy warned, shaking his head. Grace could see in his face that he was upset, just short of angry. But then she thought of the babies in the squalid house and she didn't care.

"Have you seen your father recently? Something is wrong with him. He looks terrible. I think he may be sick. Besides, it's always the money with you, just like it was on our wedding night. Why did you choose to enter Christian service if money is so important? Why didn't you simply go into business?"

He glared at her like a sulking child.

"I know Felicita, Tommy. She is my friend. What happens to her baby is my concern. You and Lester have other babies; unless, of course, they get sick and die or the authorities come knocking at your door and take them away. It is illegal to operate a *casa de engorde*, a fattening house. I'm sure you know that."

She watched his face as he considered her words; her fate and the baby's depended on Tommy's response.

"Okay, you win." Tommy finally said.

Grace sighed, and in her heart she said, *Thank you, Lord.*

"What will you do with the baby?" he asked.

"I don't know," Grace said. "But one thing is

certain. I'm not doing anything with Felicita's baby until I give the matter a lot of prayer. Something I would recommend for you also."

"I will," he replied sheepishly, "in my own way. Just remember to keep this business quiet. We don't want attention brought to the mission." He walked from the room but quickly returned holding a white envelope, which he handed to Grace. "Here. It's from Felicita. She wanted whomever adopted her baby to have this."

Grace looked inside the envelope and saw a silver medal.

"I think it's Saint Christopher or somebody," Tommy said. "Felicita was Catholic."

The house was astir that night as Grace and Marta made preparations for the baby. Grace didn't want to let the infant out of her sight. Formula and diapers were retrieved from the compound. Sam, Evie and Josh were captivated by the little girl, and gazed in awe at her tiny hands and feet. Evie fed her a bottle and burped her, while Sam set up the cradle beside Grace's bed. Later, after dinner, Grace peeked in the room to check on the baby, and she found Josh sitting by the crib, speaking softly to her. A candle flickered on the table beside him splashing large, dramatic shadows on the walls and darkening the corners. Josh and the baby's crib glowed in the candlelight, as if caught in the spotlight of time. Grace tiptoed over to stand beside him. Her heart stopped for a moment, and then started up again as she heard the old familiar words. Then she stood silently and listened as Josh, her son, turned the pages and read once more his favorite book, *Where The Wild Things Are.* Although Grace knew it was impossible, because the infant was far too young, she could swear the baby was smiling.

18
DREAMER

I don't remember much about the drive to Canoguitas because I slept most of the way. My dad sat in the front seat with the driver and practiced his Spanish while Mom and I lounged in the back seat. When we started out from Antigua, the sun was shining but the air was crisp, and I felt chilled like when biting into a cold, tangy orange. I pulled a sweater from my tote before settling into the old, black car that served as a taxi. Chico, a placid and agreeable fellow, was our driver. He nodded politely as I entered the car and then closed the door for me. Although he appeared older than my dad, he wouldn't accept help with the luggage, and insisted my father sit in the car while he loaded the trunk.

While my dad and Chico set about trying to piece together conversations with bits of English, Spanish, and pantomime, my mother studied the scenery and took pictures. She was the memory keeper of our family. She took most of the pictures in our albums and from every trip or excursion she brought home small mementos. Many of her choices seemed strange to me, and when I asked her about them I usually got the same answer: "It called to me." Rocks frequently called to her, as did feathers, seed pods, and sticks. Occasionally she acted like a normal tourist and actually bought a souvenir, but not often. I once made the mistake of accusing her of stealing.

"You're taking stuff that doesn't belong to you," I stated.

She looked stung, as if I'd slapped her in the face. "I'm a collector," she said, "besides, these things don't belong to anyone, they are just lying around waiting to be found. I'm taking them home where they belong." For her, every trip was a journey of discovery, as if the whole world was a playground strewn with misplaced treasures—things she never knew were hers until she found them waiting. Her sense of wonder at the natural world always amazed me.

As we snaked our way down the highway toward Canoguitas, the temperature warmed and I grew tired of looking at my teen magazines. I stretched my arms and yawned, contented as a cat, and leaned across the seat with my head in Mia's lap. I dozed in and out of consciousness like a cork comfortably bobbing on waves of conversation mingled with the hum of the car. At one point I heard the word *soñadora* repeated several times. "*Soñadora* means dreamer," I heard my father say. And the others softly said *yes* and chuckled.

Mia touched my hair and repeated the word.

"Soñadora." I understood they were talking about me, calling me the dreamer.

The next thing I knew, we were there, at the Evangelical Friendship Mission of Guatemala. I, the dreamer, was rising from the backseat to find my mom and dad already out of the car and being greeted by an older couple.

The couple, it turned out, was Grace and Tommy, two names I had heard my entire life. They looked older than Mom and Dad, even though they were about the same age. Maybe they aged rapidly because they were missionaries and lived in the tropics. God's work must be demanding, especially in the heat. Grace was a small woman with silver hair pulled back in a bun. She wore simple homespun clothing. Tommy was taller with a receding hairline and thick-rimmed glasses. He wore a straw hat. Both were quite thin.

Grace warmly hugged both my parents, but she seemed especially close to mom. The two of them were like school girls in each other's company, always giggling and whispering. Tommy, on the other hand, was reserved and business-like. He was mainly concerned with running the mission and talking about God. Often he would just beam, in a self-satisfied way, as if privileged to some divine secret. He usually carried a Bible and tried to engage anyone who was willing in a theological discussion. Mom and Dad listened to him because they were polite, but I tried to avoid him because theology wasn't a subject in which I was interested.

On one occasion he got me alone and asked me which I thought was more important: the destination or the journey.

"You mean our trip to Guatemala?" I inquired.

"No," he answered, "the journey of life. Have you ever thought about it, Quetzal? What life is all about? Its purpose?"

"That's way too heavy for me; I'm just a kid. I'm more interested in music," I said. "And TV, which, by the way, isn't very good here. You need to get better reception. You've only got two channels and they're both in Spanish. It doesn't give a person much to pick from."

"No," he said. "I guess it is disappointing to a young lady like yourself. But promise me you will think about my question. And if you find an answer, then come and tell me. A hint, Quetzal: the answer can be found in the Bible, as can all answers. So read your Bible, and if you read it carefully, you will find it."

"I don't have a Bible," I said. "Mom and Dad have one at home—somewhere."

"I'll get one for you. That is a promise. Everyone should have their own Bible. It is a special book, the Word of God."

****

The mission where the Tuttles lived and worked was an interesting place, with lots of buildings clustered around a church. There was a medical facility, a few out-buildings, and small houses where various people lived or worked. Several rather smallish Indians—local people dressed in the traditional Guatemalan garments—scuttled about, going back and forth between buildings. There were also peacocks which free-ranged through the compound and made strange noises. The king of this operation was Tommy's father, a very old man named Lester. We were introduced to Lester shortly after we arrived. He didn't say much. Mostly he just nodded his head. He looked about 100 years old, sitting in a wheelchair like a figure made from wax, starring out in space. His wheelchair was pushed around by a woman I first thought was hired help. Later I learned the woman was Evie Mendoza, daughter of Grace and Tommy. She carried a hand towel and would gently blot spittle when the old man drooled. The whole mission experience was surreal, like being inserted in a living postcard. But by the second day, my initial curiosity passed and there wasn't much for me to do. You can only watch peacocks in Guatemala for so long. Even gathering avocados got boring. I found the visit to the mission remarkably unremarkable and I just wanted to get back to Michigan to be with my friends and listen to my music.

One night I overheard a conversation between the Tuttles and my parents. Tommy said there never was enough money for the mission and that was why they started a sponsorship program. Dad asked what becomes of missionaries when their work is finished. "Do you have a pension or retirement plan, like a 401(K)?"

Grace answered, "We trust that the Lord will provide. We will have the knowledge that we lived our lives for Jesus. That is enough. As for accumulating material things, no, there won't be much. The mission board has a retirement home in Ohio where we can reside and live out our days with a modest allowance."

When my parents were alone, Dad remarked, "I always knew Grace was devoted to God and a dedicated Christian. She never wavered from her beliefs."

Before leaving for home, Tommy made good on his promise to get me a Bible. It was the Old and New Testaments combined and was bound in black leather. On the inside cover Tommy had

written:

To Quetzal,

A girl of whom any parent would be proud. The answers are inside—all you need are the right questions.

Jim & Cheryl Pahz

19
THE SHOEBOX

Grace looked around the room, admiring her accomplishment. Even after a year, the transformation still surprised her. The odor of urine was gone, as were the flies that had initially assaulted her senses on that horrible day. Every surface of every counter and table had been scrubbed clean and then painted either blue or white. Grace felt a sense of peace as she looked at the blue walls and white cupboards, and she smiled at the collection of clean baby bottles lined upside down on the counter top.

This whole enterprise had begun with the disagreement over Felicita's baby. Grace was adamant that the child be placed with a loving family and she wouldn't permit her husband or the mission to profit from the placement. She had called Daniel Fisher in Michigan. Daniel was an old friend from her days at Theophilus. She had run into him and his wife a couple of years earlier at a college reunion and Daniel had explained how he and his wife, Mia, suffered from infertility. They were childless and Grace had indicated she would pray for him, without realizing that someday she would play a part in answering that prayer. *How ironic,* she thought. She wondered about little

Quetzal, the baby the Fishers adopted, and how the precious child was doing. It pleased Grace to be here now doing common chores, and she felt guilty at her pleasure. But her guilt didn't last long; there was just too much to do. The house in the Rapado didn't clean itself. Even with the maids and the two live-in sisters who cared for the babies, the work never seemed to be finished.

Three times each week Grace visited the home to check on the babies and determine the work assignments. At first she spent a lot of time just teaching the girls how to properly clean the bottles and attend to the infants. She had already fired several workers for being lazy or indifferent to her instructions. She would have fired a hundred if need be; Grace wanted only dependable, loving women to care for her babies. Laundry was a big part of each day, and, unless it was raining, the house was surrounded by gently flapping white garments and diapers drying in the sun. On two days Grace brought supplies and treats for her helpers. Coffee and gum were in great demand, so she made sure they never ran out. Even Tommy appreciated the improvements she made. Nowadays he would occasionally visit with a client from overseas or a parishioner from the ministry to show off the children and how well they were treated in the foster home. But Tommy constantly reminded

Grace to keep everything low-keyed. "We don't want to draw attention," he said. Sometimes she wondered why. She was proud of what had been accomplished and the care provided the children. But then she reminded herself of the Biblical admonition from *Proverbs 16. Pride goeth before destruction and a haughty spirit before a fall.* Pride was a bad thing. Tommy was probably right. It was best to do God's work quietly and humbly.

On this particular morning in November, Grace softly sang as she folded a mound of laundry on the table in front of her. She liked participating in the everyday chores of the house. She often sang hymns as she worked. Sometimes she sang in Spanish, but today she sang in English. It was a familiar hymn from her days before Theophilus— so long ago when she was a little girl. *Blessed Assurance, Jesus is mine....* It had been a favorite of Mema's, her grandmother. When she thought about Mema, her eyes would tear. If ever there was an angel on this earth, it was her Mema, and though she was presently with the Lord, Grace missed her terribly. She had Tommy to thank for sending financial support to her grandparents right up to their deaths. He never complained and was faithful to this responsibility.

Grace grabbed a clean towel and snapped it in the air before smoothing it out on the table.

She needed to concentrate on the task at hand. The babies were napping and a slight breeze billowed the curtains making them look like sails on a boat. She heard a light tapping behind her and turned to see Vickie, one of the sisters, standing in the doorway.

"There are some people at the door asking for Señor Tommy."

"Do you know who they are?" Grace asked.

Vickie shook her head. "No. One is a woman who says she wants her baby." Then Vickie shrugged. "I've never seen her before."

Grace left the white towel in the sky-blue kitchen and walked through the house to the front door. A man and young woman stood waiting on the porch. Grace pushed open the screen door and stepped outside. "Can I help you?" she asked.

"I want my baby." The young woman pleaded with a look of desperation on her face. "Please, Señora. Is my baby here?" The man said nothing. He stood with his hands in his pockets looking down at the floor. It was obvious these two people were impoverished. The man's pants fit poorly and were stained. A piece of rope served as a belt. He was wearing a pair of black wing-tip shoes that were covered with dust. The young woman was missing a front tooth. The adjacent tooth had a gold band around the edges. Grace thought the gold band must have cost the woman a considerable sum.

"Which baby?" Grace asked. "Who are you?"

"My name is Patricia de la Cruz and my baby is Miguel. Last week my uncle…." She turned her head to her companion, who shifted in discomfort under her gaze. "He was supposed to be watching Miguel for me. But he gave my baby to Señor Tommy while I was gone. He said they made an arrangement. You wouldn't believe what my parents and I have gone through to get him to confess what he did. This is a big mistake, Señora. I would never give Miguel away." Patricia stopped to catch her breath and scowled furiously at her uncle. "You had no right to do what you did. Tell her," she hissed. "Tell her it was a big lie. Miguel is mine. I am his mother. You can't just sell him to a stranger."

The uncle looked up. "Yes, Señora. This is a bad thing I did." His hand trembled as he pulled out of his pocket a wad of crumpled bills. He held the money out to Grace. "Here," he said. "For Señor Tommy. This is what he gave me." Then he removed his watch and handed it to Grace. "He also gave me this watch."

Grace shook her head appalled. "No. Whatever Señor Tommy gave you is yours. You keep it," she said, refusing the money. "I am sure this must be a misunderstanding." Grace momentarily felt at a loss as how to proceed. Instinctively she believed these people, but she couldn't just hand a baby over without proper documentation. The uncle stuffed the Guatemalan currency and watch back into his pocket and the girl began to silently sob.

"Please," Grace said, "this can all be worked out. But Señor Tommy is not here now. I don't know where he is but I will see him this evening. I can't just give you the baby on your say-so. I don't know who you are. But if you come back tomorrow when Señor Tommy is here, we can sort this out. Believe me, Patricia, no one will take your baby away from you. For your baby's safety, I must be careful. Do you understand?"

Patricia wiped her tear-smudged face and nodded, "Yes, I understand what you say, Señora, but I want to see my baby. Can I just see Miguel? I need to know he is all right."

Grace was hesitant only because she feared that once Patricia saw Miguel, the young mother might become even more distraught or try to flee with the baby. But Grace also feared a serious wrong had been committed, and she sensed Patricia's deep concern for the welfare of the child. Finally she responded, "Yes, of course you can, but only you, his mother, may come inside. You," she said, pointing to the uncle, "must stay out here."

Grace opened the door and led Patricia inside while Vickie remained at the door watching the uncle. In the nursery, there were currently three babies in bassinets. Patricia immediately spotted Miguel and went straight toward him.

"There you are my son," she said, leaning over the bassinet to gaze at her baby. Tears began to flow again. Grace stood beside Patricia and watched as the woman nuzzled Miguel's dark, damp hair, drinking in his aroma and covering him with kisses. Miguel, who had earlier had a bath and midmorning feeding, was deep in sleep and lightly perspiring.

"See," Grace whispered, "Miguel is fine. We are taking good care of him. Look around. He is in a nice, clean room and is being well fed."

Patricia looked around at clean blue walls and crisp white sheets. On the shelf next to the changing table were three stacks of freshly laundered diapers as well as several packets of Pampers. There was enough powder, lotion, and baby wipes to care for a dozen babies, and these smells all commingled with that of the sleeping infants.

Grace lightly touched Patricia's arm. "Tomorrow. I promise. I give you my word."

"Alright," Patricia said. "Tomorrow."

Slowly Grace led her out of the room and toward the porch. Patricia moved as if in a trance until she reached the front door. Then she stopped and turned to Grace. "Please," she whimpered. "Please. I want Miguel. He is my baby and he needs his mother."

"Of course he does," Grace smiled, reassuringly. "I am a mother, too. I understand how you feel. But I need to get the proper paperwork. Tomorrow it will all be fixed. Everything must be legal. I'm asking that you just be patient for one night. That is all the time we need to check the documents and make sure everything is in order. You can see Miguel is safe and being well cared for. I promise you I will take good care of your baby. Just for tonight. That's all I ask."

Finally Patricia allowed herself to be led out onto the porch. "Thank you Señora," she murmured. "I'll return tomorrow." Then she and her uncle turned and headed toward the dented red Chevrolet that waited for them at the end of the path. Grace remained on the porch, gazing after the truck long after it had pulled away. Her body was motionless while her mind attempted to process what had just occurred.

You can't just pay for someone's baby, she thought. *What kind of trouble was Tommy getting himself into this time? The child's records will answer my questions. There has to be documentation on this baby.* Grace rushed into the back room that served as an office. Along with household and baby supplies, there was a file cabinet that contained the necessary paperwork on the house and the babies the mission cared for. Tommy and his lawyer, Mr. Cantu, were always concerned about having proper documents.

The top drawer of the cabinet held office supplies and correspondence. Files on the children were in the middle two drawers. Grace began with the second drawer and worked her way down, looking under *de la Cruz* and then *Cruz* without success. Next she tried *Miguel*, but there still was no file. *Maybe it was misfiled,* she thought, so she began reading the names on every file; still no file for Miguel de la Cruz. The bottom drawer had always been jammed, so they didn't use it. She tugged on it now to see if it would open, but it held fast. She pulled the drawer above it forward enough to check if any files had fallen below it, and was encouraged when she was able to make out something laying in the bottom drawer. To reach it she needed to empty the drawer above and completely remove it from the cabinet. This took about five minutes. That's when she found the shoebox.

Lying toward the back of the bottom drawer was an old cardboard box that looked to have been well handled. On the box was printed the word *footwear.* Grace reached in and lifted the shoebox out of the drawer. She slowly stood up and placed it on a table. She removed the lid and found the box full of letters. Many appeared to be in their original envelopes. She picked one at random and examined the writing and postmark. It was addressed to Tommy. But instead of having his correct address, the address was a post office box in Miami, Florida. Curious, she tried to read the date of the postmark, but couldn't make it out. The return address said Miss Yadira Escobar and was from Santa Barbara, Guatemala. Grace removed the letter inside the envelope and read:

"Dear Señor Tommy,

Since our wonderful weekend together it has been almost eight weeks. I worry because you said you would come back to me. Eight weeks is long time since I don't hear from you. I want tell you I packed my things ready to leave now. I told people I leave Santa Barbara, all neighbors and friends listen with sincere interest. I tell them I married now and together we live in United States because you told me so. Everyone is happy for me and filled with happiness. But I can't understand why I don't hear from you. I look for mail every day thinking maybe you had an emergency or big problem. I pray you are not sick or injured. Please write soon and tell me what need I to do. I like very much you explain me. Until then, I keep remembering the good times and love we have in sincere friendship and possible marriage. I waiting and pray that one special day you surprise me again, like other time before. You show up like in a dream to make my life better forever. It is fine with me we marry in Santa Barbara if that is what you want. But if you prefer we can marry in the United States. It is okay and not importance to me where we marry because I have no family but you to love. United States is good country too. It is important only we marry and make life of happiness and good times. Therefore decision is yours to make. I love you very much and think of you all the time. Please write soon.

Love and a thousand kisses,
Yadira Esocbar

Grace reread the letter. Yadira had printed the date at the top: September 24, 1975. That would mean she wrote this letter over ten years ago. Tommy had been married then and the father of children. It didn't make sense. Grace examined the other letters. All appeared to be from different women in several countries in Central America. There were letters from Honduras, El Salvador, and Nicaragua—but most of the letters were from Guatemala. In some cases there were photographs and several letters from the same individual; there were four letters from Yadira. Beneath the shoebox, Grace found a stack of newsletters entitled *Friends of All Nations* filled with pictures of young women who wanted correspondence for "friendship and possible marriage." *Was this what Tommy had been doing? Was he writing these women for friendship and marriage? Was he paying money to obtain their addresses? Could he still be doing it?* Grace looked at the first letter again. She had a terrible sinking feeling and her hands tingled. The letter was from Santa Barbara, under a two-hour drive from where she presently was. She was familiar with this village. She had been there before and even knew someone who lived there—a lady from the Garden Club. Grace's confusion turned to anger and she tasted bile in her mouth. She thought she might be physically sick. She knew her husband had been unfaithful. That was not a secret, but this behavior was reprehensible. It was deceptive and

240

vile. *Even Tommy,* she thought, *must have limits to his depravity.* Suddenly Grace knew what she must do. She would travel to Santa Barbara and speak with this woman, Yadira. She must get to the bottom of this today, before confronting her husband.

****

Yadira was not hard to track down. Grace and Vickie simply drove to Santa Barbara and found the house that matched the return address on Yadira's letters. Vickie waited in the car while Grace inquired within the house as to Yadira Escobar's whereabouts. Then she listened, heartsick, to the story about a young girl who had died of a broken heart. It was a sad story, like so many in Guatemala. For such a beautiful country, there was an abundance of pain and cruelty, and it seemed to Grace that the young and innocent suffered the most. Perhaps it was the same everywhere. But here, today, it was different because today Grace learned it was Tommy—her Tommy—who had delivered an unbearable sadness to a simple, trusting soul. Now that sadness was hers.

After leaving the house, Grace drove the car to the edge of town, as she had been directed by the woman of the house. Yadira's grave was not hard to spot. It was in an area reserved for the indigent or unknown. Yadira had no family, and apparently nobody cared enough to purchase a headstone. Somebody had made a crudely constructed wooden marker and painted her name on it. The paint was now faded. Grace would not be able to get the answers she had hoped for from Yadira, but that didn't matter. She knew what she needed to do. Tomorrow she would return Patricia's baby and tonight she would deal with her husband. She thought of a verse from the Bible—*And if thy right eye offend thee, pluck it out....*

20
CANCER

The worst year of my life began when Mom got sick. One morning I teased her because I thought she was putting on weight. I said she looked pregnant. But when I saw the look on her face, I immediately knew I misspoke. "I know," she said. "Something weird is going on. Lately I feel so bloated with such cramps."

"You need to go to the doctor, Mom. It might be serious."

"I know. I've just been too busy. But you're right. I'll make an appointment." Two weeks later she met with our family physician and the nightmare began. There were tests, and more tests. A gynecologist finally delivered the diagnosis: cancer. Life immediately moved into fast-forward.

Within days, Mia had surgery. They cut her from top to bottom. It was a grueling procedure that left her weak and exhausted. She lost thirty-five pounds in two weeks and had a shunt inserted in her chest to remove fluid. This was followed by chemotherapy. I watched my beautiful, vibrant mom fade before my eyes. She was brave and strong as she faced the inevitable, and her fierce determination brought out the best in me and Dad. Each day we stood by her side in battle and put on a brave front. Each day we came a little closer to losing her.

Mom had always loved to garden. In springtime and early summer, I would frequently find her in her garden digging, planting and pulling weeds. Her flowerbeds were a showpiece. After the cancer, the garden was invaded as weeds attacked with vengeance. Every day the weeds mocked us as we made our way between the house and car to keep her appointments at the treatment center.

As I accompanied Mom for her medical care, I realized there were many other people like her; people whose lives were interrupted by cancer. One day there were about ten women sitting in the waiting room. They all wore different colored turbans on their heads and they reminded me of the flowers in Mom's garden. That night after I returned home, I sat at my desk and wrote a poem in my journal.

The Cancer Garden

They sit covered by turbans.
Each head wrapped in a different color.
Pastels and bright bold shades
of pinks and blues.

Pretty patients
who glance around the room.

Eyes dart like humming birds
trying to solve a puzzle.

Some read last year's magazines
others gaze
but all search quietly.

Absolute silence.

Tulips in a garden.

Waiting to see
if spring will arrive.

From that day forward, I visited Mom's garden every day to take care of the flowerbeds she could no longer tend. Pulling weeds was a way I could honor my mother.

Although her garden bloomed and arose from the weeds, my mom didn't. All Dad and I could do was watch helplessly while the cancer overtook her. When she was first diagnosed, I felt disbelief. Cancer happens to other people. Mom had always been so strong and healthy. Then, as she began to shrink before our eyes, I became angry—with her for being sick, and with myself for being so helpless. I was angry with Dad, but I didn't know why. Then, following Mom's passing, I became angry with God for letting her die and leaving me alone. It seemed so wrong and unfair. She'd gone through the surgery and chemotherapy. She lost her hair, and did everything the doctors asked of her. She suffered and then she died. It was senseless and wasteful and I kept asking, "Why?"

Why would a just God let something like this happen? People would say to me, "You shouldn't blame God. He has nothing to do with it. He created the universe and then stepped back to let it run by itself. The universe runs through natural laws. What will be will be." Yeah, maybe! But I wondered, *What about miracles? When did God quit performing those? What about the people healed by Oral Roberts, Ernest Angley or other television evangelists? What about the pilgrims who go to Lourdes in France? And then there's the church in Antigua, Guatemala, that has walls lined with crutches, canes, and thank you notes to Brother Peter for interceding with God and causing miracles to happen. The notes were from hundreds of people who supposedly were healed. Was Mom any less deserving? Did she need intercession? Would the outcome have been different if we visited Lourdes or Antigua? I doubted. In fact, I came to the conclusion that all such miracles were fake, and the men who performed them were charlatans.*

They say you don't appreciate what you have until you lose it, and I know that's true. But it's not because of a lack of trying. My dad and I both tried to cherish every moment we had with Mom during the final weeks. We savored the good days, and when they became fewer and fewer, we savored the small moments—the soft touch of Mia's hand, her understanding smile, or just sitting by her side and watching her in peaceful sleep. But neither of us could comprehend the huge, dark hole that her absence would leave in our lives. When she died, the landscape of my interior world changed. It was as if my heart had been struck by a meteorite and had been left scorched. I lost my best friend and confidante. I lost someone who would always love and accept me, no matter what. I felt like a garden without sunlight. Without Mia's warmth, the world was cold and colorless and stretched before me and Dad like an endless winter. We might have stayed in that winter forever if not for my baby, Maya. Maya would laugh (or cry) and for a few moments winter's spell was broken.

Gradually I came to realize that the way I could most honor my mom was not by tending her garden or surrendering to grief, but by living my life and caring for those I love—my father, and my wonderful baby girl. Once I realized that, life became easier and thoughts of Mom were about happy memories. Even though Mom is gone, I still feel her presence every day. It's as if she is always in my house, but just not in the same room I'm in. Even though we're not together, it's comforting to imagine her here with me—always just one room away.

Condolence cards arrived for weeks after Mom's passing. Dad kept them stacked neatly at Mom's end of the bedroom dresser. After a month passed, I offered to help Dad clear out her drawers and the closet. I knew it would be difficult for him to go through her clothes and personal items by himself. We worked together for about ten minutes before he had to excuse himself because he was overcome with grief. I wasn't sure what to do with the condolence cards, so I decided to store them in a box and discuss it with Dad later when he felt better. As I sorted through them, one caught my eye. I opened it and saw that it was from Grace and Tommy Tuttle. There was a handwritten message inside which read:

> Daniel – my heart breaks for you and Quetzal, I know this must be such a difficult time. I worry for Quetzal—for a second time she has lost her mother. I pray she does not lose faith. It was an honor to know Mia and to call her my friend. You and Quetzal will always have a special place in my heart, and you are always in my prayers.

It was signed Grace and Tommy Tuttle, but I knew the message was strictly from Grace. I remembered the trip my parents and I took to Guatemala and how happy my mom and Grace were together. Just thinking of the sun and vibrant colors of that land brought a warmth to my spirit. I would give anything to revisit that time and hear my mother's gentle laughter. Suddenly I felt compelled to visit Grace and Tommy's mission. I wanted to reconnect with Guatemala, for myself and for Mom. This time I would experience it through different eyes and perhaps I could learn more about the two most important women in my life—my two mothers.

21
THE RECKONING

After three days in jail, Tommy was desperate. *What happened? Where is Grace?* He had assumed he would be out a day ago. *What is taking so damn long?* The dark cell was cold and damp and made his bones ache, but it was a hundred times better than the first cell he was put in. He was originally incarcerated with five other men who were not friendly to gringos. They glared at Tommy with contempt and stole his food. His lawyer had managed to do something right; he arranged to have Tommy transferred to a cell of his own. Now Tommy was alone, except for a Bible and one bold rat that scurried past his doorway several times a day as it went about its business. Tommy sat and contemplated his predicament. He was astounded and outraged. Even the lowly rat was better off than he was! The rat had a life and could come and go as it pleased; Tommy was the one trapped. *How could this have happened?*

He was brought out of his thoughts by a guard who announced a visitor. The guard looked to be fourteen years old and carried an automatic weapon. A second guard opened the cell door and instructed Tommy to hold out his hands. As the guard spoke, he showed no emotion, and he didn't return Tommy's smile as he put on the handcuffs. "Follow me," he said as he turned and left the cell. Tommy obeyed and heard the guard with the gun walking behind him. *Lord,* he thought. *You'd think I was a criminal.*

Tommy expected to see his attorney, Mr. Cantu, or Grace in the meeting room. Instead, he was surprised to find Francisca, his wife's friend and lawyer—the one who had helped the Fishers with the adoption of Felicita's baby. But Tommy didn't question the strangeness of the situation or even how Francisca knew he was in jail. He was happy to see anyone. "Francisca," he said, "I'm so glad to see you!"

Francisca smiled weakly, and motioned for Tommy to sit down. Then she turned to the closest guard. "Please," she said, "remove his handcuffs. He is not a danger to me, and you will be right outside the door." The guard undid the handcuffs and then left the room, closing the door behind him. Before the door completely closed, Tommy saw the young guard with the gun take a seat in the hall outside the door.

"Francisca," he said, "thank goodness you are here! Have you seen Grace? Can you tell me what's going on?"

"You don't know?"

"All I know is what my attorney, Jose Cantu,

told me two days ago. The mission and the house in the Rapado were raided. I'm accused of buying babies for illegal adoptions. It's all a bunch of lies, but now the police, or judges, or someone wants money. Jose told me I have to pay ten thousand dollars in cash, through him of course. He will get it to the *right people*. We don't have that kind of money, Francisca. I told Jose I can't pay that much and I haven't heard from him since. Thank God you've come. I need someone I can trust. How is Grace? Is she okay?"

"Grace is fine," Francisca answered.

"Good," Tommy said. "That's good. Can you get me out of here?"

"Actually, I'm not here as your attorney, Tommy. I came to deliver this. Grace thought you might need it." She placed his *Scofield Bible* on the table, the one he received from Grace on their first anniversary. It had a green leather cover and his name embossed in gold letters.

Tommy stared, dumbstruck. "Not another Bible!" Then he leaned forward and pushed the book aside. "Where is my wife? Why hasn't she come to see me? Does she know that Cantu wants ten thousand dollars?"

Francisca sat and calmly watched as Tommy's fury bubbled to the surface. He knew it was unwise to lose control, but he could barely help himself. All he wanted was answers—a few simple answers—and then to be released from this horrible place. Tommy sprang up and began pacing the room in agitation. He looked in the mirror. He assumed he was being watched from the other side, but he didn't care. He was startled by the image reflected back at him. He saw a man who looked dirty and disheveled, tired and defeated. He must be dreaming. That sad little man couldn't be him… Tommy Tuttle… the Assistant Director of the Evangelical Friendship Mission of Guatemala. Tommy ran his fingers through his hair and pulled, as if to awaken himself from this bizarre nightmare. But nothing changed. He was still here, caught in a drama he didn't understand. He slowly turned and returned to his seat.

"I'm sorry," Francisca said. "What transpires between you and Mr. Cantu is privileged. He is your attorney. I represent Grace, and she won't be coming to visit. She and the children have left Guatemala. I am not certain when or if she will return. If you wish, I can forward her something—a letter or message."

"What?" Once again Tommy was caught off guard by his circumstances. Just when he thought things couldn't get worse, he received another blow. "What do you mean? Where has Grace gone?

She didn't say anything about this to me. Doesn't she realize the trouble I'm in? She's got to help me get out of here!"

"I'm sorry, Tommy, but that's not possible. Grace is the one who put you in here. She and the woman whose baby you purchased."

For a moment, Tommy forgot how to breathe. He slumped into his chair and then he felt himself fall forward onto the table. When he was finally able to take a breath, he realized he was sobbing, totally defeated, like a child. He felt Francisca's hand on his and looked up into her sad, dark eyes.

"Woman? What woman are you talking about?"

"A woman named Patricia de la Cruz. Her infant son, Miguel, was taken without her permission. You are charged with buying Miguel for 500 quetzales and a Casio wristwatch." She took out a newspaper clipping and placed it on the table between them. "A *casa de engorde,* Tommy. It says you were running a fattening house. You've made all the Guatemalan newspapers and I understand you also are in some papers in the United States. Lila is in custody, too. All the children have been confiscated."

Tommy placed his head in his hands. As the anguish inside him steadily welled, his fingers curled to grip his hair until at last it seemed his hands were all that kept the whole top of his head from exploding. He looked up at Francisca, his hands still holding his head. "This is absurd," he said. "Grace wouldn't betray me on the word of a... some stupid woman."

"Betray is not the word I would use, Tommy. I'm sure Grace did much praying before she contacted the authorities. It was a difficult decision for her. Sometimes a person has to do what is right, even if they don't want to. Sometimes God speaks to their heart." Francisca reached into her jacket pocket and pulled out a handkerchief which Tommy gratefully accepted. "Tommy," she said softly, "I wonder if you have accepted Jesus Christ as your personal Savior."

"What?" Tommy was dazed.

"Are you saved Tommy?"

"What do you mean *am I saved*? Don't you know who I am?"

Francisca slowly shook her head. "I'm not asking who you are and I'm not talking about lip service. I know you have read the Bible and can quote scripture. You are good with words, and I'll bet your words have been effective on people. But I wonder, what about you? What about your soul? Have you ever turned to the Lord and accepted His gift of salvation? Have you personally opened your heart and asked the Lord Jesus to come in? If you haven't, I believe now is a good time. We all fall short of the glory of God, Tommy, no matter who we are. But you… well… you have misused your talents and gifts. You have hurt those who love you and put their trust in you. And, you have made a mockery of the God you claim to serve."

As Tommy listened, his hands slowly slid to his lap. Then he watched Francisca remove some tattered envelopes from her pocketbook, and place them on the table in front of him. He recognized the letters immediately, and flinched at the sight of them.

"Do you know there is a woman in Santa Barbara who is no longer alive because of your lies? Grace went to visit her and she was told the woman died from a broken heart. Yadira was her name. She died while waiting for her lover, a gringo named Tommy, to return to her as he had promised and marry her. It's all here in the letters."

Tommy remained silent. He didn't answer Francisca because he couldn't. There was no answer. He was no longer in a jail in Guatemala. He had fallen into another place, a place he suspected was hell. Tommy had hit bottom; and yet, as he pondered this turn of events, he experienced an unexpected clarity of thought and vision. Finally, after what felt like an eternity, he spoke: "I am a contemptible man. I am beyond forgiveness."

From a distance he heard Francisca's voice, and he was flooded with gratitude that another human being would deem him worthy to address. "Nobody is beyond forgiveness. Christ pardoned the thieves on the cross. If He could forgive them, He can forgive you, Tommy—even you. All you have to do is ask the Lord to come into your heart. If you are truly sorry, He will see it. You can fool people and you can fool yourself, but you can't fool God."

Francisca rose and walked until she stood beside him. Then she took Tommy's hand and knelt down so that her face was close to his and he could smell her perfume and the remnant of the breath mint she had eaten after lunch. "Let's pray together," she said.

Tommy bowed his head and began to pray. Francisca's hand was like a lifeline, and as he prayed, Tommy felt himself being pulled out from hell. As he ascended, he let go of everything he was ashamed of—the whole pack of lies that was his life. Yes, he was a liar, a cheater and a manipulator. He had used people and hurt others for his own pleasure and personal gain. He admitted all this, and then he turned his back on it. Tommy let go and immediately felt lighter, no longer tethered to his sin. It was a wonderful sensation, like a feather riding the breeze—a beautiful green feather like that of the quetzal bird. The struggle was over. He was a feather that rested in the palm of Jesus Christ, his Savior. Tommy asked for and received the gift of salvation. Now he had to forgive himself and he knew that would not be easy.

Before leaving, Francisca took out a piece of paper from her pocket and wrote down some notes. "I want you to look up these verses," she said. "Study them. Being saved is a first step, but if you are a Christian, a true Christian, you will want to live your life differently. I don't believe it's too late for you, but you have to make some changes. These verses may help you take your first steps."

Tommy accepted her paper. "Thank you for believing in me."

Back in his cell, he read the verses Francisca had written. *She's a lot like Grace,* he thought. But he didn't mean this in a derogatory way. *There are good people and bad.* He knew what he had been. *I want to be good*, he thought. He opened his Bible and turned to the first verse Francisca had written, *James 2:20: "But wilt thou know, o vain man, that faith without works is dead."*

Jim & Cheryl Pahz

22
HOME

Christmas was only a week away and there were still a lot of presents to wrap. Grace was behind in everything. She just couldn't keep up, but she knew she would somehow manage to get everything done. She always did. She tried not to think of all the chores waiting for her at home as she and Tommy drove down the mountain to observe what had become a tradition. They rode in silence. This was the fourth trip for Grace. Tommy had come only the previous year. On the first two trips, Tommy was not free to come. He was in prison.

When they reached their destination, they left the car and walked together in silence. Tommy held a small bouquet as Grace led the way to the new location of Yadira's grave. The headstone Grace purchased three years ago replaced the boards that had originally bore the young woman's name. The stone still looked new and polished, and was an elegant memorial. On its surface was carved the message: *Beloved of God. Rest in Peace.* Tommy placed the flowers at the foot of the headstone and then stood as he wiped away a tear. "It's me. I'm here again," he whispered. "I'm so sorry. Please forgive me." Instinctively he reached for Grace's hand. Together they scanned the horizon as if waiting for a response. The view from the new location was beautiful, and the only sound was of waves rushing to the shore. Beyond the cemetery was the vastness of the sea, while behind them were mountains covered with lush green forests. Grace took several deep breaths, inhaling the peace and beauty that surrounded this place. She was satisfied she had truly picked the perfect spot for Yadira. "You are with Jesus now," she said. "You are safe. You are home."

****

Sam and Evie were waiting as Josh and their grandfather cleared Guatemalan customs. Lester walked with a cane now, and he was the last passenger to pass through the gate. As soon as he emerged with Josh at his side, Sam and Evie were there to give him a hug. Once Lester caught his breath and was steady on his feet, the four of them walked out of the airport. As they left, they passed under the large banner that read: *Welcome to Guatemala... Land of Eternal Spring*.

Outside, Josh paid the boys who carried their luggage and helped the driver load the bags into the car. Josh was a handsome man with wavy black hair and serious brown eyes. He was robust and strong, in contrast to Lester who was pale and gaunt. But even though Lester looked as old as his years, he was still animated; his eyes were lit with excitement.

"We had a wonderful conference at Theophilus College," Lester said enthusiastically. "Just glorious. And several distinguished evangelists were in attendance. I gave my testimony and souls were saved. I believe we really are getting our reputation back. Praise be to Jesus! The Bible says a good name is rather to be chosen than great riches."

Josh closed the car trunk and walked to Lester's side. Lester continued taking to Sam and Evie. "I never could have gone to Nashville without the help of Josh. Your brother is my rock and a Godsend. I kept forgetting things, but Joshua was there to remind me what I was supposed to do or where I needed to go. He kept me on course," Lester chuckled, "like a pilot of a ship—or rather, an old and rickety boat." Lester paused. "I don't believe we'll ever do adoptions again, but I don't think we should. I should never have let you father talk me into the adoption business in the first place. It was a bad idea from the start."

"There are lots of other things we can do, Grandpa," Evie said in a soothing voice. "There are other ways to serve the Lord. That's what Mom always says. She says that serving the Lord is our number one priority. That's why you started the Friendship Mission, Grandpa."

"You're right, sweetie," Lester smiled. "There are many ways to serve the Lord, and we will never be short of work."

Between having a stroke, Lila's disappearance, and the adoption scandal, the last four years had been hard for Lester. But what had distressed him most, was the fear that the ministry he had spent a lifetime nurturing might be destroyed by Tommy's behavior.

Lester's desire to restore the good name of the ministry is what helped speed his recovery from the stroke. It was not easy to regain the confidence and support the program had lost. The publicity from the adoption scandal had been terrible. Tommy was convicted of buying babies and sentenced to prison. The future of the ministry was jeopardized, and Lester was shamed by the actions of his son, even though he, Lester, was a silent conspirator. Seething with anger, Lester was ready to turn his back on Tommy and curse the day his eldest son came back into his life. But reason and compassion prevailed. How could he curse the son who had given him Evie, Sam and Josh? And what about Grace? She was now like a daughter to him. His other children had left the ministry and lived separate lives. Maggie was married to a businessman in Honduras and Miguel taught mathematics at a college in California; Lester seldom saw his youngest children. Tommy, Grace, and the grandchildren were his family now, and he feared if he lost Tommy he would lose them all.

The first few weeks that Tommy was in prison had been torture for Lester. He returned from the hospital with no family to help him. Lila had disappeared and Grace fled Guatemala with the children. The stroke left his right side partially paralyzed. He had difficulty with simple, daily tasks like eating and dressing, and he could barely walk with crutches. A few loyal servants remained at the mission to assist him, but Lester felt as if his world was crumbling around him. In desperation, he called Francisca, Grace's attorney and friend, pleading for Grace's telephone number. Francisca refused, but she did contact Grace with the request that Grace please call Lester. He was so overjoyed when Grace called the next evening, that he burst into tears and begged her to return with the children to the mission. "I'm so alone," Lester said. "Please, Grace, I don't want to die here by myself."

Tearfully, Grace replied that she was concerned for him. She was uncertain that he would want her back because of all that had transpired. She said she and the children loved him and were homesick. They were ready to return home.

The week that Lester waited for their return seemed intolerable. He was depressed and found it difficult to sleep. He couldn't concentrate on anything except having Grace and the children in his life again. He had not felt such heartache since he was a young man in prison and learned his first son, little Joey, had died.

When Grace returned to Guatemala, she worked wholeheartedly with him to reestablish the mission's reputation. Each small victory gave Lester a renewed sense of purpose and brought meaning to his remaining years. Gradually things improved with both the mission and Lester's relationship with Tommy. When Tommy was first released from prison, Lester didn't want him associated with the mission. Only after much prayer and discussion with Grace did he finally agree to accept Tommy back. Grace convinced Lester that forgiving Tommy was an opportunity to put their Christian principles into practice. Both Grace and Lester believed that Tommy's religious conversion in prison was genuine and they welcomed him back into the family and the ministry.

Each day Lester thanked God for the miracles in his life. *There is no life without setbacks and disappointments. What I had almost lost, I have now regained, and in some ways life is better than ever.*

Tommy was now a better husband and son since returning from prison. *It shows that good things can happen when God is invited into your heart.* Lester wasn't worried about Tommy any more.

"Come on, Grandpa," Evie said. "Mom and Dad will be back from Santa Barbara. Everyone will want to hear about the conference in Nashville."

Lester paused. He had to move slowly—deliberately. But he felt good today. He smiled as he inhaled the acrid air of Guatemala City, and noted the traffic congestion. It was so familiar. Street kids begged arriving passengers for loose change. Off to the side, a few children stood with eyes half closed, and swayed to the internal rhythms of their intoxication. *Resistoleros,* Lester thought; *glue sniffers.* How many times had he preached against the insidious practice? Still it continued. *Not much has changed,* he thought. *The place is as gritty and noisy as ever.* He took a deep breath and turned to Evie. "It feels good to be home," he said. "I can't wait to tell your parents how successful Josh and I were at the conference. And, by the way, young lady, I hope your shopping is done. You know, it's almost Christmas."

Jim & Cheryl Pahz

23
THE PATHS WE CHOOSE

When I arrived in Guatemala for my second visit, I was met at the airport by Grace and Tommy. They looked as I remembered, but older. Tommy seemed a bit smaller than I recalled, and he was now completely bald. Grace was unchanged except she had more wrinkles and her hair was silver. She wore it pulled back in an untidy bun, with stray flyaways arching around her head like a halo. The two of them, standing side-by-side, reminded me of the couple from the *American Gothic* painting by Grant Wood. After welcoming embraces, we put my luggage in the trunk and Grace instructed me to sit in the front passenger seat. Tommy climbed into the back while Grace slid behind the wheel.

It felt odd to be back in Guatemala, following the same route I had traveled with my parents thirteen years ago. The city was still loud, vibrant, dirty, and colorful. Through my eyes it seemed more chaotic and raw. I wondered if this impression was real or simply due to the fact that I was older now with a greater interest in the world and the people around me. As I absorbed my surroundings in all their assaulting beauty and grime, Grace chatted cheerily. Tommy sat straight-backed and rigid in the back seat, occasionally humming or reciting a

Bible verse.

When we left the city and entered the countryside, Grace focused on me. "It's wonderful to see you again," she said, turning her gaze from the road and smiling broadly. As she turned her face back, I noted a sadness, quick and unexpected like when a cloud passes in front of the sun. "We were so sad to hear about Mia. She was such a wonderful person, an angel. I shall truly miss her." Grace's eyes looked ahead, but I could see tears ready to spill. Then she took her right hand from the steering wheel and reached for mine, squeezing it gently. I willed myself not to cry and squeezed back.

"Thank you," I said. Then we both quietly composed ourselves and stared at the road ahead, seeking refuge in the future and our destination.

Gradually the mood changed and Grace spoke. "How's your father doing?" She asked.

"As good as can be expected, I guess. After forty years of marriage, it's a big adjustment. He got pretty run-down taking care of Mom toward the end, and then he became depressed. Right now he seems to be getting better. He loves being a grandpa, so I left him in charge of Maya. She wouldn't stand for anyone else taking care of her. Next to me, my dad is Maya's favorite person. They are real pals."

Grace laughed at this. "Daniel always was a pushover for babies, especially cute ones. I'll never forget when he first saw you. We met him at the airport and Mia brought you. You couldn't have been more than six months old. Anyway, all it took was one look and your dad was a goner. It was love at first sight."

"That sounds like him and Maya," I said. "I'm hoping that spending so much time with her will lift his spirits. He loves being with her, and she keeps him too busy to think about the past. He won't have time to get broody."

Grace smiled and nodded as I spoke. "It sounds like Daniel is in good hands, and I'm sure he'll do fine. He's going through a transition, but he'll make it. He just needs time."

"I know you're right," I said. "It's just that I worry about him." Then I tried to explain the reason for my visit. Grace listened patiently as I talked. At the conclusion I said, "I guess I'm here to pick your brain. You're the only person I know who's known both of my mothers. For some reason it felt important that I come here and talk to you about them. I know it doesn't make a lot of sense."

Then Grace scolded me gently. "Dear child, don't be silly—it makes perfect sense, and I'm so glad you're here. But tell me, and please be honest because I'm not judging you, do you think you might have come here to find Felicita?"

I was reflective for a moment, feeling stupid and stunned. Of course that's why I was here, although it truly did not occur to me until Grace uttered those words. Finally I responded, "Yes, I guess that might be part of it—at least to know if it would even be possible. I'm not sure how much you know about Felicita, or what you remember."

Grace sighed. "I remember Felicita well. I can see her in my mind as clearly as yesterday. She was such a pretty girl, just like you. She came from the city of Mazatenango. Of course that was a long time ago, and I don't think the mission kept good records at that time. As an organization, we were in our infancy. At any rate, Mazatenango is probably a good place to start. A good strategy might be to put up a poster and check local court records. It's too bad Mia isn't here with us to share in this adventure. Your mother always wondered if you'd be back one day to learn more about your past. She asked if I'd be willing to help if you ever expressed an interest. Of course I assured her I would. Your mom always wanted the best for you, and she worried about every little detail, like when your dad named you Quetzal.

"I remember the moment he named you after you were born. I was talking to him on the telephone, and told him we needed a baby's name right then because the doctor was filling out the birth record. Immediately he came up with the name Quetzal. 'Name her Quetzal,' he said. I was surprised because I always thought of that word as the Guatemalan currency or the bird; never did I think of it as a name. Mia told me she was a little concerned at first, too. She loved the name but worried it might prove to be a burden to you. But she trusted Daniel's instincts, and then, as soon as she saw you in person, she knew your father had chosen well. She had the chance to change it during the adoption, but she wouldn't consider another name for you. She was right. Daniel picked the perfect name. Each time I see you, the name fits you better; it's as if you've grown into it. And just look at you now! You're all grown up with a child of your own. Where does time go?"

From the back seat I heard Tommy say, "What is man, for his days are like grass...." But he wasn't really talking to us. He was simply narrating the scene. During the whole ride to Canoguitas, he recited phrases—usually Bible verses—like background music to our journey.

"Tell me," Grace said, "about Maya. I hope you have some pictures."

"Of course," I responded, as I proceeded to dig in my purse for the collection of photos I always carried with me. And for the remainder of the drive, I bragged shamelessly about Maya, describing what a beautiful child she was, and how well-behaved and intelligent. "It must be those good genes I got from my parents," I joked.

****

For several days we searched for Felicita. Besides myself and Grace, there was Joshua, the Tuttles' oldest son, and the driver of the car who was a quiet man of Mayan descent. The driver proved to be quite helpful speaking with the local population. Joshua was tall with wavy black hair and intense dark eyes. He also had a quiet nature, like the driver. However, I sensed our driver's quiet demeanor was due to shyness and a sense of innate humility. Joshua's silence seemed the result of his desire to be precise and respectful. Joshua was always contemplative before giving an answer or offering an opinion. He had a logical, straightforward manner that was smoothed over by an easy smile and sense of humor. I found him immensely likable and was glad it was Joshua who accompanied us instead of Tommy with his back-seat monologues.

"You know," Josh said as we rode in the car the first day, "I used to rock you when you were a baby. I read you stories."

"Yes, I know." I answered. "You told me that on my last visit."

"Yeah, but you were a rebellious teenager then. I wasn't even sure you were listening. I'm only teasing. You weren't bad at all. Really."

I saw Josh was concerned he had offended me. "Thanks," I responded, "but I remember how I acted on that trip. I was really obnoxious. I don't know how anyone put up with me. But my turn will come. I've got a daughter of my own now who's growing up so fast, she'll be a teenager before I know it. Then I'll be in trouble. You know what they say, *what goes around comes around*."

"Yes, I know." Joshua rolled his eyes and proceeded to share the latest escapades of his children. I hoped someday Maya would have the chance to meet Joshua and his family

****

After spending the better part of the week searching, it appeared we were not going to locate Felicita. We inquired of numerous officials, put up posters, and Grace checked at the courthouse. Nothing worked. We received a few tips; vague reports of someone who might have been Felicita, but nothing substantial. Either Felicita had moved from the area long ago, or she didn't wish to be found.

"I guess it's not meant to be," I said, after five days searching. I felt guilty about the time my project was taking from these people who put their lives on hold to indulge me. "I feel like a failure. I expected it would be easy to find her."

"You tried your best," Grace remarked. "No one can do more than her best. I have an idea, let's take a day or two and change focus. I think we could all use a holiday. I want you to go home with some happy memories. Tommy and I know a lovely place where we can relax, listen to music and enjoy terrific food. That way, when you return home, you will have something pleasant to talk about."

"That sounds wonderful," I said. "I've really enjoyed seeing the countryside, and you've all been so kind and patient. But I have to admit, I'm tired of hunting for a ghost. A day or two of relaxation would be great."

So the next day, Tommy and Grace took me to a resort in Tiquisate. It was named *Paradise Gardens* and was adjacent to a beach. It was a beautiful facility with fabulous accommodations surrounded by green lawns and gardens, and an Olympic-size swimming pool. In the trees, colorful parrots sat squawking at the guests. We spent the first day lounging around, soaking up the sun and walking through the gardens. Tommy sat apart in the shade, reading his Bible. He seemed perfectly content to be lost in his reading, sipping lemonade. Occasionally he would look up to make a comment to Grace and me or quote a Bible passage. He would then immediately return to his reading. In the evening, we listened to a concert performed by several marimba players and three different mariachi groups.

On the second day, I decided to swim. The water felt wonderful, and even though I was getting anxious to return to Michigan, I was happy that Grace had suggested this holiday. I pulled myself out of the pool and plopped in a chair across from Tommy. I felt as relaxed as a turtle basking in the sun. The experience was delicious. Tommy wore a bathing suit and a short sleeved shirt with palm trees on it. He had a new straw hat and looked like a tourist. He didn't have his Bible today.

"Why don't you try the water, dear," Grace said. "It looks refreshing." Then she turned to me and said, "I hope you're enjoying yourself, Kat."

"Oh yes," I responded. "This is wonderful."

"I'm sorry our search failed," Grace said. "But it was an adventure."

"It didn't fail. Like you said, it wasn't meant to be. To be honest, I don't really know what I was looking for. I don't even know what I'd say to Felicita if we found her. I am starting to get homesick and I'm ready to get back to Michigan."

"In my opinion," said Grace, "everything happens for a reason. It's all part of God's infinite design. We've seen this in our own lives, haven't we Tommy?"

Tommy mumbled an inaudible response, and stared at me so long that I began to feel uncomfortable. Finally, after several moments, he spoke: "I'm sorry you weren't able to find you real mother, but it's been a long time. She probably moved out of the city and lives somewhere else. Who knows? Anything could have happened to her. It's something we'll never know." And that, apparently, was all of the conversation Tommy wanted to make. He leaned back in his chair, sipped some lemonade, and then turned his face toward the sun.

Without knowing it, Tommy had struck a nerve. There are two words that when thoughtlessly used send me into a tizzy. One of the words is *real*, especially if it is linked with mother or father. I suppose that is part of the legacy of being adopted. I didn't say anything, but I was irked by Tommy's reference to Felicita as my *real* mother—actually more than irked; it made my blood boil. What was Mia—my unreal mother? Felicita birthed me and placed me in these people's hands, but she was no more real to me than my memory of the tooth fairy from when I was a child. The truth was that Felicita was a woman who got pregnant and gave me away. She may have had noble motives, but the fact remains she didn't raise me. She didn't sit by my bedside when I was ill with a fever. She never went to parent-teacher conferences, or took me to Girl Scout Camp. She didn't drive me every day to school or pick me up at the end of the day. Felicita may have been my birth mother, and she was quite likely a wonderful person, but I never considered her my real mother. My *real* mother was Mia Fisher, and I resented Tommy for his insensitivity. He knew my mom—the person I had recently lost. His lack of respect for Mia seemed a slight to her memory, not to mention their friendship.

The other word that I'm sensitive about is the word *adopt*. It's frequently misused. I get annoyed when people say things like they want to *adopt* a puppy, or when they decide to clean the highway and *adopt* a stretch of road. Such figures of speech bother me. One man I met in Guatemala, a music director, referred to the church's choir as *his adopted children*. Such talk makes me want to scream. Why do people misuse language so thoughtlessly? Mom used to say I was too sensitive. "What's the difference?" she asked. "It's no big deal." But to me it is. I think the idea of adoption is diminished by stupid expressions, no matter how well-intentioned. Adoption involves love, commitment and sacrifice, just like marriage. Both are sacred. But you don't hear people say, "I married a stretch of highway." Why do people feel free to toss the word *adopt* around like a Frisbee?

Periodically I let loose with a tirade on such thoughtless remarks, and I considered whether I should explain my feelings to Grace and Tommy. Would they understand or would they be offended? I already had the sense that Tommy resented me and the time he spent away from his program. I was sure this whole vacation was at Grace's insistence. Before I had the chance to speak, Grace touched my hand and asked if I wanted a tropical fruit drink. "Sure," I said, and a waiter immediately brought us two drinks made with pineapple, coconut, and banana. It was tasty, and as I sipped on my drink, and listened to the mariachi group stroll through the garden, my irritation subsided.

"I think I will go into the water," Tommy said. He removed his hat and shirt and plunged into the pool. I watched as he swam a few laps and then floated on his back. Minutes later he climbed out of the pool and walked to his chair.

Grace said, "You know, Quetzal, I once gave Mia a notebook that Felicita had left. Did Mia ever give you that book?"

"Years ago," I answered slowly.

"I always wondered about that book and hoped you'd get to read it someday. It must have been special to Felicita."

"It's special to me, and something I treasure," I said. "That and a Saint Christopher medal she left. I cherish them and keep them in the wooden box I bought on my first trip to Guatemala. Her book is filled with her writings: poems, recipes, magic spells, and random thoughts. For example, she wrote about when to plant for a good harvest, or what steps to take to find true love, or how to get revenge on a cheating lover. Some of her things I still can't understand because they are written in Quiché, but the ones in Spanish I was able to translate."

"I believe she left the book on purpose, for you to have. She was a sweet girl."

"On the last page of the book," I said, "she wrote one verse I believe was intended for me. I translated it as:

Fly away little bird.
My nest is empty.
How far will you go?
What wonders will you see?
Fly away little bird.
My heart is empty.
You take with you my dreams.

"That's beautiful," Grace said.

Then Tommy, who had just emerged from the pool and was drying himself with a towel, said, "Quetzal, are you saved?"

"What?"

"Do you know Jesus as your personal Savior?"

"Well," I answered after a long pause, "I am a spiritual person. Sometimes I go to church, but not much."

"That's not what I asked. Do you know Jesus personally? Do you walk and talk with Him on a daily basis?"

"No," I answered, "not really."

"Do you know what we do here, Kat? I mean at the mission, when not hunting for lost birth mothers? We are in the salvation business. That's our purpose. We exist to lead people to Christ. God has sent you an invitation. Read John 3:16. It was written for you and for me."

"Thank you," I said. "I appreciate your concern. And I'm sorry if I've imposed on your work at the mission. I know what you do is important, but you really don't need to worry about my salvation. I might not walk and talk with Jesus like you do, but I believe in God and welcome Him in my life. As long as we're being candid with one another, I must tell you I'm uncomfortable with some of the things you say. For instance, your use of the word *real* coupled with my mother. My mother was Mia Fisher and she was very real to me."

"I'm sorry, Quetzal. I spoke without thinking; a poor choice of words. Forgive me, but then what are you really doing here? Why are we looking for Felicita if she isn't real to you?"

I was surprised, because he had asked a good question and I wasn't sure how to answer it.

Tommy continued, "All I ask is that you give some consideration to the welfare of your soul. Where will you spend eternity?"

"Tommy, I'm not worried about eternity. My family is not religious in the way you are. I was taught to look for God everywhere—in churches, temples, even in nature—most of all in nature. My dad once conducted an experiment. He called it *ten churches in ten weeks*. We tried ten different houses of worship in a row. I was a senior in high school at the time, and I really resented having to get up early just to go to some new church. But Dad and Mom insisted, and in the end it was an interesting experience. Of all the places we tried, one of my favorites was a Buddhist Temple. It was peaceful there; we stared at a wall and meditated. There was no pressure and I found the experience uplifting.

"You know what I got from Dad's experiment?

Not a whole lot at first. But over time, I've come to believe that God doesn't live in a church or place. God lives in each of us, we just need to learn how to recognize Him. You don't go to church to find God; you take God with you to church and spend time there together. I don't mean to be disrespectful, but my idea of God is different than yours. I'm happy with my spiritual life, in the same way you are happy with yours."

Tommy sat back in his chair and shook his head. "Salvation is not a matter of being happy, Quetzal. Idiots are happy. Even a dog can be happy. Happy does not equal right. Do you ever wonder about the purpose of your life? What is your destination? Believe me, you won't get to heaven by staring at a wall."

The word *destination* elicited a memory. I thought for a few seconds and was taken back thirteen years to my first trip to Guatemala.

"I remember now. You asked a question when I visited here with Mom and Dad. You asked me which was more important—the journey or the destination? I did think about your question, and I believe the journey is more important. That is the answer I get from meditating. I accept myself and seek to be the best person I can. I try to live my life by the golden rule. In the end I will get the destination I deserve. That is karma. We always get the destination we deserve."

"You are incorrect." Tommy was adamant and I could tell he was irritated. "The right answer is the destination is more important. It determines which journey you will take. For a true Christian, the destination is heaven, and getting there defines the journey."

"Perhaps, but I might not be a true Christian, at least not by your standards. I don't have a formula; I'm open to all possibilities. I don't think your idea of God is the only right one. It might be right for you, but not for me. I think the Bible is an ancient text, filled with history, parables, and mythology. But I don't believe it is literally true. Surely you don't believe the Bible is literally true?"

Tommy was passionate as he responded. "Absolutely. Every word is inspired! There are no errors. That is what inerrancy means—without errors. The Bible is a map you can follow to get to your destination."

"There's that word again," I said. "Destination."

"You are a liberal and a secular progressive," Tommy said, "Smug and prideful. The Bible says *pride cometh before destruction and a haughty spirit before a fall.*"

"I am content with the path I have chosen."

"We are all sinners and come short of the

Glory of God," Tommy replied. "That includes you. You need to be saved from your sinful nature."

"I don't regard myself as much of a sinner. I'm human, like you. We aren't supposed to be perfect. Only God is perfect. Sometimes I eat too much or I procrastinate, or I say something insensitive and hurt somebody's feelings. If these are sins, karma will deal with me in the appropriate way. I think faith is a deeply personal matter that lives in a person's heart. It is not for display and I don't wear it on my sleeve. My beliefs are not based on a payoff with a reward in an afterlife. I don't even know if there is an afterlife. I hope there is; I want there to be one because then I can be with Mom again. But I live my life for the present. I try to do my best because it feels right and I want to make the world a better place—to make a contribution. But regarding sin, don't you think some sins are worse than others? And what about mistakes? Is a mistake a sin? For instance, the adoption scandal you were involved in years ago—was that a sin or did you make a mistake?"

Tommy reflected a moment. He seemed taken aback. "I haven't done an adoption in almost thirty years. Not since...." He paused for a moment, and then continued, "You know that I have been in prison?"

I nodded. "I read a newspaper clipping from a

long time ago that I found in a drawer of my mom's bureau. I think it was from the *Miami Herald*."

"That was the worst time of my life. I never sank lower," Tommy said. He lowered his head and then raised it and looked directly at me. "That was a complicated time, Quetzal. I went to prison because my bad judgment led me to sin. It wasn't a simple, honest mistake that put me in jail; it was pure, full-blown sin. But I was redeemed. I have been washed in the blood of the Lamb. Jesus pulled me from the pit of iniquity. I've done some terrible things—shameful, selfish, things. I will never forgive myself for what I did. But Jesus forgave me."

"Was my adoption one of those terrible things?"

"No, of course not! Even a sinner is bound to do a few things right."

"So, you are no longer doing adoptions?"

"Lord, no. Part of my parole agreement was that I would never do adoptions again. But I wouldn't have continued with them anyway. I learned my lesson. I didn't need an order from the authorities telling me what to do. You see, when I emerged from prison, I was a Christian, probably for the first time in my life. I had been born again in Jesus Christ, and since that time I have a peace that passes all understanding."

"I see," I replied. "I am happy for you. Truly, I am."

"Then maybe you can understand my concern—my motivation. If you don't get saved, you will be lost forever. It's not too late, Quetzal. Read your Bible. First read it with your mind, then with your heart. You must be born again." He turned to Grace. "Isn't that right, Grace?" There was pleading in his tone, like a salesman who can't understand how you fail to appreciate the value of the deal he is offering you.

"Yes, Tommy," she said, and then reached out and held his hand. "That is our belief."

Suddenly I felt sorry for the Tuttles, this gentle and well-meaning couple. They had treated me with such kindness and patience. I remembered how, during my first trip to Guatemala, I overheard Grace talking to Mom and Dad about their mission work and the prospects for their future. There wasn't much of a retirement provision for them. "God will provide" was how they summed up their future. I remembered thinking at the time that they were denying reality, playing ostrich, and burying their heads in the sand. Now I found myself reconsidering. There was no denying they had found something—an answer so profound that looking toward the future posed no threat. The future didn't concern them.

I'm being argumentative, I thought. *I am trying to show how clever I am. But I'm not clever. I'm ungrateful and unappreciative. Tommy's right, I am full of pride.* I felt ashamed. "I'm sorry, Tommy," I said. "I know you are sincere in your beliefs and I appreciate your concern for me. When I get home I'll talk to my dad about this. He went to Theophilus, and I'm sure he will have something to say. He loves to talk religion. In fact, he's the only person I know who actually looks forward to visits from the Jehovah's Witnesses."

And that was pretty much the way we left things—theologically speaking. Tommy asked if I still had the Bible he gave me on my last visit. When I answered yes, he looked pleased and told me to read it. I promised I would.

That was the last thing Tommy said to me about religion. We returned to the mission, and the following morning I was on a flight back to Detroit.

24
BEYOND SPRING

The trip home to Michigan from Guatemala was a long one, and gave me plenty of time to think. I left the airport in Guatemala at 6:00 a.m. and wouldn't get out of Detroit's International Airport until past midnight. But through the different stages of my flight, I had time to reflect. I was a different person from when I had left my Michigan home.

When I said farewell, I hugged Grace and Tommy. I felt this might be the last time I would see them. I wondered about Tommy. Was he really a man of God, or was he just used by God to achieve some greater purpose? I didn't know. But standing in the waiting room of the airport, I realized I had not come to the *Land of Eternal Spring* to find Felicita; I had come to make my peace and let her go. This was where she belonged and where she would always be. Elusive, like the bird I was named after, her spirit would inhabit the cloud forests in the same manner she haunted my dreams—an invisible yet powerful presence that thrives in my imagination. There would be no need to return because part of Felicita was within me and always would be. She would remain the shadow-mother that still haunts my dreams and whispers to me in my sleep. I wondered where she was now; what she was doing. Was she writing poems? Perhaps she is the one who called me back to Guatemala through one of her spells, pulling me out of my slumber to a true awakening of the person I was intended to be; the person I needed to find. Maybe she knew, if I came to Guatemala looking for her, I would discover myself.

And what of my mother, Mia? She is the light that illuminates my world. Her light allows me to glimpse Felicita as she wanders through the shadows of my imagination. Mia illuminates my path, and guides me home like a beacon. Her light will never fade.

As the airplane headed toward Miami, I saw that I was leaving one world (my Mayan past) to embrace another (my American future)—just like when I was adopted so many years ago. Only this time, I was alone and fully aware of what awaited me. As I thought of Maya, my body ached to touch my daughter and hold her near. I wondered how I ever could have left her for a week and concluded I must have been crazy. Then I thought of my dad— my real dad—and I was overcome with longing to see him, and talk to him, and hear his laughter. I realized that these two people are the center of my world. They are my village and I am the weaver. With threads of memories and magic, I am weaving a design large and beautiful enough to hold my family and all our dreams for as long as I am here until one day I disappear like those before me. Like the bird I was named after: the Quetzal of Guatemala.

The End